Dusky
Embrace

DUSKY EMBRACE

First edition. July 2, 2024.

ISBN: 979-8227335951

Written by Ava Arinna Ginsburg and Areen Ahmed Muhammed.

A Novel

Dusky Embrace
A Novel by both
Areen Ahmed Muhammed
Ava Ginsburg

Dusky Embrace
A Novel by both
Areen Ahmed Muhammed
Ava Ginsburg

A Novel by Two Authors from Two different Continents

Public Library Cataloging-in-Publication Date
ISBN:

Printed in

Areen Ahmed Muhammed [*]©
Ava Ginsburg [*]©

Dusky
Embrace
By

Areen Ahmed Muhammed
Ava Ginsburg

Dusky Embrace
Authors: Areen Ahmed Muhammed & Ava Ginsburg
Novel
Year of Publishing: 2024

"No one can LOVE ones, but all can remember the First LOVE."

– Areen

"As we let our light shine, we unconsciously give other people permission to do the same."

– Ava

To

    ME, YOU, and ALL Those Who Search for LOVE

Words To Be Remembered (PREFACE)

In 2023, Dr. Areen Ahmed Muhammed asked if I wanted to write a book with him collaboratively. We would start with a novella, a shorter book, at first. I had never written a book before whereas he has written quite a few, but I knew for a fact we both share a profound love of reading books. In fact, one of our first conversations, before we were best friends, was when I told him I read 'Naguib Mahfouz's *Palace Walk*' and he asked if I wanted to walk with him the next day to a second-hand bookstore in Wuhan, China back in 2018.

On that fateful rainy day, I quickly learned how special and funny and smart Areen is. It feels as if we started a conversation in 2018 that has thus continued to this day. We wrote a film script then and the excitement that ensued when we finished writing it was unlike I have ever experienced before. Areen continues to inspire me to see what I and we can accomplish. I am incredibly grateful he is in my life and I cannot wait to see what we write next. I love him to the moon and back and well into the next galaxy too.

This novel is truly one of a kind. It is unique. But that makes sense, because I am unique, and so is Areen. It blends American and Kurdish cultures and transcends the boundaries of language, culture, and borders. This novel is a bridge between us. It is about reconnecting with an old friend and all that accompanies that– values, the frustration of time zones, and longing, but also courage, bravery, persistence, and happiness. It is about a friendship that ages like fine wine and can withstand a long amount of time apart. It is a work of fiction that I hope some of you can relate to. Writing is challenging but I got a lot out of it.

We poured our heart and soul into this one. We hope you enjoy reading it as much as we enjoyed writing it.

- Ava

As far as we have the beginning, then, definitely, we should have an end...

Chapter One

<u>Avan</u>

Avan is standing in her bedroom in her West Loop 3rd-floor apartment in Chicago, Illinois at dusk. All her clothes, mostly black, are sprawled across her queen-sized bed. The sun momentarily eclipsed her window from the row of brick apartment buildings that lined her street. It is shortly before Christmas and Avan is cosy in her soft turtleneck sweater and bunny slippers. Since her apartment complex was old, it was always a bit drafty, so Avan was always wearing a sweatshirt, sweater, or jacket, even in the summer. She despises being cold, to the extent that her friends finally stopped thinking that she was not just being dramatic, that she really was a petite flower, or petite fleur, as the French call it. It was old but absolutely one of a kind, with honeycomb-shaped black and white tile on the bathroom floor, original wood engraved trim, a clawfoot bathtub, a Murphy bed, high ceilings, and decorative crown moulding.

From the 3rd floor, she is far away from the snow that covers the streets, cars, and roofs like a fluffy white blanket. A few intrepid neighbours are already out there, shovelling the sidewalks. Avan furrows her eyebrows as she looks from her clothes to the empty rolling suitcase (hardshell) next to them, and past that to a postcard-sized invitation glaringly situated on her desk, as if it was in the spotlight. It is a wedding invitation to her cousin Hannah's wedding. In Italy. On Valentine's Day, February 14th. *There are worse ways to spend Valentine's Day, I suppose*, Avan thought. *Oh, Hannah*, she mutters to herself. She looks around her bedroom, suddenly noticing all the details of her space. She and her cat are ensconced, especially with the recent installation of orange shag carpeting, much to the chagrin of her landlady. Although, underneath the carpet is gorgeous pine hardwood floors, so technically the shag rug is just there to protect them. There is a corkboard above her desk with playbills, audition calls, and awards thumbtacked to it. She has acted in everything from Shakespeare to West Side Story. Her mousepad is a miniature Persian rug. A stack of books and plays crowd her slightly broken cheap IKEA desk. Her bedside lamp is a leg lamp, a miniature version of the one from *A Christmas Story*.

Avan goes to her desk to sit down and take a sip of her hibiscus tea, now no longer searing hot. A wave of uncertainty suddenly goes everywhere in her body, like a glass of spilt milk that is accidentally knocked over. It permeates in her, increasing her heart rate. She is not sure about the trip or travelling when there is snow or leaving her cat, Muffin, behind. Even if the trip is only a few days. She is conflicted. Avan opens her laptop, taking a minute for her eyes to adjust to the brightness of the screen. She goes into her email and finds the last one Hannah sent her. It says, "You are welcome to bring a +1 with you. I cannot wait to see you soon, Aves." Avan's heart sinks. *I should go*, Avan thinks to herself. *I cannot miss Hannah's wedding. She is the first cousin in the family to get married. And when will I have another opportunity to travel to Italy?* Hannah is one year younger than her, yet here she is, getting married first. Avan sits with that thought for a minute, feeling a bit guilty for feeling competitive, as if finding love has a timeline or is a competition. This is not about her, it is about Hannah and Nick, Hannah's fiancé. Who was she to feel otherwise? Why does she still feel this way? Avan takes out her phone and opens Contacts to find her friend Amy who lives in West Virginia. Not paying attention to the list, she clicks the name Aaron by mistake, putting the phone on speakerphone. After hearing Muffin's meowing from a distance, Avan heads to the kitchen to feed her cat who up until a few moments ago was sleepily stretched out on the floor, lost in the pleasure of a cat nap. *Ppst ppst pst* Avan calls as she sets Muffin's gourmet cat food on the floor. She pets Muffin and lets her eat dinner. Avan returns to her bedroom, leaving the door open for her cat to come and go when she pleases. The phone keeps ringing as Avan patiently waits to leave a message. She takes off her glasses, rubs her temples, and picks up her phone. She reads the name 'Aaron' and her eyes widen in shock. She immediately hangs up. This is her old friend who lives in Sulaymaniyah. Not Amy, her dearest friend in West Virginia, confidant, fellow lover of ice cream, corgis, and British mystery television shows. Avan abruptly gets up, she is caught off guard and starts folding a few of her clothes and organising them in her suitcase to distract herself.

There is a pile of her best-quality clothes for the Italy trip and a pile she will put back in her dresser and on wire hangers in her closet. She opens the closet and fishes out a flowing lavender dress, feeling the fabric between her fingers. Muffin, meowing, comes trotting in from the other room. She scoops Muffin into her arms and pets her. After a couple of minutes, she goes back to folding clothes and re-dials Amy's number, relieved to hear her friend's bubbly voice on the other end of the line.

"Hello? This is Amy."

"Amy, Darling, long time no talk!"

"Avan!! Is that you?"

"Why yes it is. How have you been, how is everything in West Virginia?"

"Same old. Everything is great."

"I was actually calling to see if you were free for a few days around Valentine's Day. My cousin Hannah is getting married and the wedding party is going to be in Venice, Italy. Would you like to come with me as my plus one?"

"Oh my gosh! Italy! How romantic. What a dream. I would love to, but unfortunately, I need to stay here with my pet hamster Bruce. I also sometimes watch my nieces after school, and they are too little to stay home alone. I totally wish I could go and I cannot wait to hear about how the trip is."

"No worries at all, I totally understand. Next time?"

"You betcha."

"Oh, Wait, then can I bring the cat to be with you? I want to have a break and travel somewhere. Would it be fine with you?"

"Yeah, sure, leave her with me and spend as much time as you wish. No worries about her at all."

"You are so sweet, thank you. Will not forget a souvenir or a postcard for you too when I come back."

"If so, then your request is accepted. Bye for now."

Avan hangs up the phone, feeling a mixture of bitterness, wonder, pain, and ease. She should have found a date for the wedding sooner, seeing as how it is an overseas trip. And now here she is, just a few weeks before the wedding. To be totally honest, she is fine being single at the moment. It is her family that is always shocked and worried that she is single. Like there is something wrong with her. Avan decides to go out and get some crisp winter air.

After putting on a myriad of clothing layers and her turquoise puffy winter jacket, she races down the 3 flights of her building's spiral staircase and steps out into the winter night under the yellow streetlights. Luckily, the sidewalk is shovelled, and there does not seem to be any ice. She thinks about how many years have passed without seeing Aaron. She wonders what he is like now, if he has changed, if he remembers her. Her boots make a crunching sound on the sparkling snow. She thinks about the memories with him, and that brings a rosy colour to her cheeks and a soft rainbow orb to her mind's eye. Nothing can attack her, not even this bitter, frigid wind. She wraps her scarf more tightly around her. No one is outside at this hour. Everyone is sleeping. Only her boots, the wind, and a landscape of snow. It is rather peaceful outside, maybe she should come out here more often. Realising it is after midnight and she has a lot to do tomorrow, she hoofs it back to her home. This is the first time she does not notice too much how cold it is, there is a lot she is preoccupied with thinking about. She climbs the three flights to her apartment, jingles the keys, opens her door, and immediately loses the layers of clothing like a snake. After brushing her teeth and washing her face, she climbs into bed. She nestles under her down comforter and breathes slowly in and out.

The next morning, Avan shimmies into the kitchen to make coffee and toast an English muffin. The whirring of her coffee maker always scares the bejeebies out of her cat. Her cat, Muffin, has already walked across her face this morning to wake her up. She wondered if all cats are crazy, or just hers. She turns on the radio station, 91.5, National Public Radio (NPR) and the familiar sound of reporters and local news fills the air with the reality of this brand-new day. Avan plugs her phone in to charge on the kitchen counter. She does a double take. On her phone screen is a missed call and a message from Aaron: "Hello there... Did you call? Call me back once you are available." She does not have time to respond to his message then, but cannot believe they are in touch again after all these years. There is an electric sort of feeling that is running through her all day as she brushes her hair and warms up her car. She drives to her play's rehearsal with a pensive look on her face. Inside the auditorium, her colleagues are doing vocal exercises and stretching. She is more patient with them than usual. She lets them all out early so she can return home to finish packing.

She drives slowly, avoiding the streets where the snow is not ploughed. A few snowflakes are seamlessly falling and disappearing into droplets of water on her windshield. The weather makes all the drivers nicer, or so Avan wants so desperately to believe. She is looking forward to her trip. She is excited to go abroad and have an adventure. With or without a plus one to the wedding, life goes on. It takes her five tries to parallel park her 2001 Oldsmobile Alero car, but she is determined not to fail. And not to hit or scrape the surrounding cars.

After she parks, she sits silently for a minute and yanks her nearly mangled hand out of her mitten. She dials Aaron's number. Her car is as warm as a toaster. Again, it rings and rings and is never picked up. Avan sighs, playing with the earrings she is wearing. She writes out a message to him: "Looks like we are playing phone tag. Tag, you are it." She checks on her phone to check what time it is in Sulaymaniyah and yelps. *Great, now he probably hates me for calling him at 4:00 am. Nice.*

The next morning Avan gets up at 5:00 am and takes the 81 bus west, transferring to the blue line train toward O'Hare International Airport. Barely anyone is on the train at this hour. Her hair is messy and there are bags under her eyes. The fluorescent lights at the airport burn her pupils. Like a zombie, she navigates the airport. It is like a maze. She has a month to enjoy Christmas Break and New Year's before the wedding party itself. The world is her oyster.

Amidst the vast expanse of the airport terminal, where the symphony of arrivals and departures resound, the young Avan seeks solace within the confines of a cosy coffee shop. She has a few hours before the flight to New York City so she heads to Pete's Coffee to grab a hot black coffee. Seated at a polished wooden table, her mind dances with thoughts of a certain boy, their connection and the enchantment of Christmas, all weaving into an intricate tapestry of emotion and longing. She awaits, taking a sip of black coffee, the steam rising from it like a plume of smoke. With every sip of her steaming cup of velvety coffee, her thoughts pirouette through the realms of memory and hope.

Her attire, a reflection of her discerning taste and innate elegance, envelops her like snakeskin. A coat of sumptuous cashmere, swathed in a hue reminiscent of the twilight sky, cascades gracefully down her lithe frame. Its collar, a sculpted masterpiece of meticulous craftsmanship, frames her delicate neck with a regal air. The fabric embraces and whispers secrets of warmth and opulence.

Beneath the resplendent coat, she dons a sweater of delicate knit, spins from balls of merino wool. Its colour, a soft blush reminiscent of dusk, mirrors the rosy tint that graces her cheeks. The sweater, with its form-fitting silhouette, embraces her slender figure with an understated allure. Each stitch, lovingly placed, narrates a tale of comfort and sophistication, harmonising with the gentle rhythm of her breath.

Her lower half adorns in tailored trousers, meticulously tailored to accentuate her graceful curves. Fashioned from a blend of virgin wool and silk, they drape her legs with a fluid elegance, invoking an ethereal grace reminiscent of ballerinas in flight. The fabric, a tactile symphony beneath her fingertips, conveys a sense of luxury and refinement. Every crease and fold align in perfect harmony, the whisper of their meticulous artistry that has commenced their existence.

A slender belt, crafted from Italian leather, encircles her waist, a subtle accent that adds a touch of sophistication to her ensemble. Its polished buckle, adorned with an intricate filigree design, gleams with a quiet grandeur, speaking volumes of the meticulous attention paid to even the minutest of details. As she sits there, contemplating the mysteries of love and the allure of the approaching festive season, the belt serves as a gentle reminder of the unity between her physical form and the garments that adorn it.

Completing her ensemble are shoes that embody both style and comfort. Ballet flats, crafted from the finest Nappa leather, cradle her feet. The material stretches to the contours of her arched feet, offering support and grace with every step she takes. Their deep ebony hue, reminiscent of moonlit shadows, complements her attire with an understated elegance that echoes her quiet charisma.

In this haven of caffeine and contemplation, Avan finds solace as she sips her coffee, her mind adrift in a sea of thoughts and emotions. Her attire, carefully chosen and meticulously curated, becomes an extension of her very being—a tangible expression of her refined spirit and impeccable taste. The ensemble, a living canvas of fabric and colour, tells a story of a girl seeking connection, her heart entangled with the thoughts of a boy and the magic of Christmas.

In the bustling atmosphere of a vibrant Pete's Coffee, her thoughts are inexplicably drawn to the enigmatic presence of Aaron. The aroma of freshly brewed coffee wafts through the air, mingling with the whispers of her musings, as her mind embarks on a journey of introspection and longing with every sip of the back coffee in front of her in a red and green Christmasy cup.

Avan, a woman of profound intellect and captivating grace, possesses an allure that transcends conventional beauty. No wonder why she became an actress and dramatist. Her eyes, deep pools of hazel, shimmer with an ethereal glow, their depths reflecting the kaleidoscope of emotions that tugs at her heartstrings. A cascade of chestnut curls frames her countenance, every strand seemingly conspiring to capture and amplify her allure. This would be a shred of clear-cut evidence of why Avan chose to be a birdwatcher in the wild and ignited her desire.

Clothed in an ensemble that spoke of elegance and discerning taste, Avan effortlessly commands attention. A tailored light blazer, in a muted shade of charcoal grey, hugs her slender frame with an embrace that whispered of sophisticated power. Its structure traces a path of precision and authority, mirroring the strength and depth of her character.

As Avan sits there, gazing into the abyss of her coffee cup, thoughts of Aaron swirl within her mind. His enigmatic smile, his eyes that held the secrets of a thousand constellations, haunts her thoughts like a cherished melody. The symphony of emotions that welled up within her becomes entwined with the very fabric of her ensemble, an intricate dance of longing and anticipation.

In that coffee shop, amid the amalgamation of voices and aromas, Avan finds herself captivated by the interplay of memories and dreams. Her attire, a reflection of her essence and cultivated taste becomes a tangible extension of her soul. In the depths of her contemplation, she yearns for a connection with Aaron, their spirits destined to intertwine in a dance that traversed the realms of possibility and longing.

Amongst the flurry of travellers at the lively airport her heart is imbued with a wistful yearning for a Christmas and New Year's Eve adorned with romance beside Aaron and her memories with him. Her thoughts drift like delicate snowflakes, dancing with the promise of love and enchantment, as she envisions a celestial tapestry of passion waiting to unfurl.

Her presence is a mixture of grace and allure. Eyes like pools of velvety chocolate glisten with the luminosity of stars, captivating souls with their tender depths. Silken tresses, the hue of midnight cascades, frames her countenance in a beguiling allure as if whispering tales of moonlit rendezvous.

Perched on the precipice of imagination, she envisions a rendezvous under twinkling lights, wrapped in a cocoon of warmth and affection. The vision of an ethereal dress, a gown woven with stardust and dreams, adorns her mind. Each stitch, a testament to the finesse of a master couturier, would cradle her form with the gentlest embrace as if the very fabric were a lover's touch. She tells herself *Wait, why are all my thoughts so complicated and I cannot think straight while I am sitting and sipping this bitter black coffee?*

In the embrace of Christmas, while she is waiting for her plane and the gate to be opened, people are sharing laughter and mirth, their hearts connect like stars in the night sky. A feast of flavours dances upon their tongues, evoking a sonata of pleasure as they revel in each other's company. Beneath the shimmering lights of the airport, they exchange glances that speak of a love profound and everlasting. If anyone would have a glance over at her, they would directly know how lonely she is now by herself. No one knows what kind of ideas and thoughts are flying like a mockingbird over her head. All they see is a lonely girl sipping her coffee all alone.

As the Eve of the New Year approaches, the traveller's connection blossoms like a celestial flower while waiting for their planes but maybe not her; nobody knows what she is waiting for. Is it Christmas itself? Or the journey she is heading toward? Or just running away from the coffee-like bitterness in her life. Inside the warm airport's bustling setting, couples are taking a moonlit stroll, hand in hand, hearts entwining like ivy climbing up a fence. Each step would create a rhythm of togetherness, as they revel in the promise of a new beginning.

With the clock's hands drawing closer to their flight times, their souls embrace the timeless magic of the turning hour. Between the departing and arriving flights, they find solace in each other's presence, as if the world conspires to unite their spirits. And as the first notes of *Gate B17 is Now Open to Boarding* resonates, they would share a kiss that transcends time, declaring their love an unbreakable seal.

On the stage of the airport's fleeting space, Avan's heart soars, knowing that love could bloom even amidst the transient spaces of modernity. The airport, a stage for comings and goings, has become the very sanctuary where her dreams of a romantic Christmas and New Year's Eve unfold.

With each passing moment, Avan's anticipation grows, and her heart beats as an orchestra of emotion and hope. In the airport's labyrinthine corridors and Pete's Coffee shop, she feels a connection that surpasses geography. With unwavering faith, she knows that amidst the comings and goings, her destiny may manifest, uniting her with the soul meant to adorn her Christmas and New Year's Eve with the ethereal beginning of eternal love...

Chapter Two

<u>Aaron</u>

Aaron, whom most teenagers in his neighbourhood know as Mr Aaron, a maths teacher at a secondary school for gifted students in Sulaymaniyah, Kurdistan, Northern Iraq, is sleeping soundly in his comfortable bed. It is four o'clock in the morning. Finally, he is on Christmas Break. No more papers to grade, parents to meet with, midterm exams, make-up tests, or office hours or particularly verbose co-workers who are eager to catch a glimpse of his personal life while he is in the teacher's lounge pouring himself a tall mug of black coffee. No more chit-chat while he is just trying to *finish a cigarette in peace.* He is wearing fleece pyjamas and wild hair. He is drooling on his pillow. It is totally dark in his room aside from the street lights outside and the occasional car that cruises past, its distant shadows dancing on his peaceful face and across his pillowcase. Finally, he is getting a good night of beauty sleep. In his peaceful slumber, he is free, soaking up the feelings even in his dreams. His curly hair proudly displays itself across the length of his pillowcase, totally unable to be tamed. His eyelashes are long and thick. He has high cheekbones. He is a dreamboat. His window is cracked open, and a cold windy breeze from the mountains that encircle his city enters his room, cooling off his feet that are sticking out from under his goose-feather duvet. Nothing can compare to this bliss. Even though he is relieved to have a much-needed break from teaching, he will surely miss his students and their youthful exuberance.

In the far right corner of his room, there is an acoustic guitar upright on a guitar stand and a guitar pick. Even in the dark, it is distinguished. It is his proudest, most secret hobby yet. Aaron relishes the challenge of learning a new song, his fingers getting blisters as he practises the chord progressions. He will play in front of an audience someday, but not yet.

Next to his bed on his bedside table is a lamp, a book, (*The Hobbit* by J. R. R. Tolkien with a bookmark from North Carolina University, U.S.A. in the middle of it sticking out) his glasses, his phone, a ballpoint pen. Suddenly, his phone screen lights up and his phone vibrates. Who could possibly need him at 4:00 am? Sleepily, he picks up his phone and blinks. ... *Avan?* He is receiving a call from his old friend Avan. He has not spoken to Avan in several years. He stares quizzically. He is confused. He puts on his glasses to ensure he reads the name correctly. It takes him a minute to register everything. He is stumped. He rolls over back to sleep.

The next morning, Aaron wakes up and smiles, biting his lip. He writes out a text to Avan: "Hello there... Did you call? Call me back once you are available." What a way to start Christmas Break– with a mystery. He starts to boil water to make coffee in his French Press, setting down his new mug, a gift from one of his students. It is cheesy and reads: "World's best maths teacher." Aaron is not so sure about that. He looks up and out his kitchen window, which is adorned with a piece of colourful stained glass. The light from outside is scintillating in his big, brown eyes. Sulaymaniyah is a beautiful, natural place. The winter is cold and the summer is hot. After opening his refrigerator, it dawns on him that he is out of milk. He is going to have to venture out to buy some milk, not very far but a close market to him named Agha.

After he puts on his winter jacket and wears his Levis Jeans and orange All-Star Converse sneakers he walks down the road toward all the shops, he contemplates what else he is going to need. He feels effervescent that the semester is done. There is a solo trip he has planned to Egypt, but his thoughts are elsewhere. He needs to buy milk for the coffee, naan bread, black tea, brown sugar, cooking oil, and some toast for his Nutella and peanut butter morning snack. Now that the semester is finished, he has time to shop. He warmly greets the shop owners that he sees and wishes them a Happy Christmas Break, though they are still working up until the day before Christmas. However, people in his country do not usually celebrate Christmas as a feast, but rather as a short Winter Break and to spend some luxurious family time. They ask about their children, cousins, nieces, or nephews that are in Mr Aaron's maths classes, and how they are doing. Aaron says all his students are shining stars, which is from the bottom of his heart. He picks out a box of black tea and wonders if Avan now drinks tea, or if she is still a coffee addict like he is. He remembers the laughs and jokes they once shared and it is as if his whole heart was set on fire. The trip to Egypt dwindles in his head against his better judgement.

When he returns home from the souq, a very small neighbourhood market, he sets his heavy backpack down on his kitchen table and unpacks the milk, then the brown sugar, tea, eggs, naan bread, freshly baked toast, and olive oil. He pours himself a mug of coffee, adds some milk, and then goes to his front porch steps and takes a seat. The region where he lives is gorgeous and mountainous. From his front porch steps, he can visibly see the mountains; especially Azmar Mountain. It is old and comforting and a landscape from his childhood. He inhales the mountain air. He remembers Avan, who was once his other half. His bitter half, they used to joke. The one and only. His sun, his moon, his trees, his heart. Being separated from her, he suddenly felt sharply in his soul, like living without this pure mountain air. He checks his phone to see if she has responded. Not yet. On the other side of the world in America, she is probably sleeping. *Should I forgive her for waking me up on my first day off after the semester ended?*

Aaron goes inside because it is getting a tiny bit windy and cold. A dusty old map of Egypt is unfolded on his desk. He begins to map out his trip to Egypt. Can a maths teacher be a romantic? There is so much with love that is impossible to figure out, like certain maths problems. There is no exact equation or formula or process to really ever know if someone loves you. There is no logical explanation for Aaron's feelings. It has been years since he talked to Avan. For the first time in ages, his emotions are stronger than his logic. He is imbued with wistful nostalgia, imagination, and hope. Avan has his number saved in her phone, so she does remember him. But does she hold the memories of them as close to her heart as he does? Does she also feel that he is her soul mate, as he so fiercely does? Does she cry when she thinks about how much she misses him? *It is a miracle our paths crossed,* Aaron thinks. He drinks another sip from his coffee and will soon pack a bag for Egypt. But before Egypt, he should spend some time in nature and away from the world. Indeed, he needs some alone time and to be by himself in a shack far away from civilisation, far away from the bustling city and cars. Far away from wires, power lines, and telephone poles. Far away from the noise and car carbon emissions. Far away from his red pen and scoring grades.

From the window of his room, a cup of coffee is in his hand and he is standing. Aaron's gaze traverses the expansive horizon, drinking in the ethereal beauty that lies before him with every sip of the coffee in his hand. Azmar Mountain, with its stoic grandeur, rises like an ancient sentinel, guarding the secrets of time within its stony entrance. The mountain's peaks: Goizha and Qaiwan, shrouded in mist and veiled by the murmurs of bygone eras, appear as if they were touched by the divine hand of a celestial sculptor. He thinks about his city, Sulaymaniyah city, the capital city of Kurdish Culture, the twin sister city of Tucson, Arizona, in America and Naples in Italy, nestled at the mountain's foothills, which exudes an aura of captivating charm. Its architectural tapestry weaves a tale of cultural resilience and historical significance, unravelling in each meticulously crafted edifice. The city's bustling streets, paved with the echoes of countless footsteps, stand as witnesses to the ebb and flow of civilizations that have graced these lands for centuries.

As sunlight filters through the lace-like curtains of the room, bathing the scene in a soft, golden glow, Aaron observes the rhythm of life unfold beneath his windowpane. The vibrant bazaars adorned with a kaleidoscope of vibrant textiles whisper tales of trade and commerce that have flourished since time immemorial. The melodic calls to prayer waft through the air and ears of Aaron, crying on the wings of faith and devotion, resonating with the ancient mosques that adorn the city's skyline. Each minaret, a testament to the architectural prowess of eras long past, stands tall and proud, proclaiming the enduring legacy of Sulaymaniyah's rich history. Aaron looks at his Rolex wristwatch, it was a present from one of his friends, and it is a bit after noon. It is the noon prayer which is why he hears *Allah u Akbar* from the speakers in the minaret of the mosques.

As the sun beams among the black clouds settle over the land, casting warm hues across the landscape, Aaron's heart swells with gratitude for the privilege of witnessing this beauty from the comfort of his room. It is a living testament to the timeless allure of Azmar Mountain and Sulaymaniyah City, a symbiotic dance between nature's splendour and humanity's creative spirit, forever entwined in the present moment.

He waits for the prayer to finish and then he says his prayers to be answered by His creator. Still, he sips from his coffee and says his prayers from deep in his bones. *I cannot wait for my prayers to come true, my mom always told me to not share my prayers with anyone so they can be answered. Oh, Mom, how much I miss you...* Aaron whispers to himself in front of the window, standing. He leaves the coffee mug by the bullnose square edge of the window. He is off to the bathroom basin to wash his face and wash out all his sadness with the cool water.

He leaves his lonely room and heads out to walk on the empty streets. A few droplets of rain pour over his coat and curly hair, but he never surrenders himself to be handcuffed to an umbrella and under the mercy of an umbrella. He likes the rain to give him another dimension of meaning in life. His ideas about this break and where to go sprout like turves grow under the merciful rain.

All of a sudden, memories of Avan hit his brain like thunder. As Aaron meanders through the vibrant city streets, his thoughts consume him with the captivating presence of Avan in an imaginary world, his cherished spiritual friend, gracefully striding beside him. Aaron starts to think about Avan as if she is present side by side with him and he goes into a deep thought while visualising Avan with himself. Avan, a living testament to the enduring allure of beauty, exudes an ethereal charm that transcends the present moment, echoing the enchantment of ages past.

Her flowing locks cascade like a midnight waterfall, framing a countenance adorned with delicate features reminiscent of classical sculptures, evoking the timeless grace of ancient goddesses immortalised in marble. Her eyes, celestial orbs, radiate depth and wisdom of bygone civilizations, mirroring the secrets of epochs long forgotten.

In his thoughts, Avan's every movement resonates with an elegance reminiscent of an era as if she was a reincarnation of a noblewoman who grace the courts of history. Her steps, measured and poised, seem to trace the footsteps of regal figures who shape the tapestry of human events with their indomitable spirit.

Amidst the bustling throngs of people, Avan's spirit stands out like a rare gem, drawing the gaze and admiration of passersby. Her presence ignites a spark of inspiration, conjuring visions of legendary heroines who influence the course of civilization. In her stride, one glimpses the echoes of historical figures whose legacies continue to reverberate through time.

As Aaron contemplates Avan's extraordinary allure, he marvels at the power she holds over hearts and minds. Like the revered muses of antiquity, she embodies the very essence of artistic inspiration, leaving a profound impact on those fortunate enough to cross her path. In her, he witnesses the convergence of beauty and history, a testament to the enduring influence of remarkable women who shape the narrative of humanity.

In this present moment, as Aaron walks side by side in the shade of Avan's shadow, and memories through the lively streets, he finds himself in the presence of a living embodiment of timeless grace and historical significance. Avan's soul's glowing presence illuminates the present with echoes of the past, a captivating fusion of beauty and historical resonance that leaves an indelible impression on his soul and steps.

Aaron walks among the resplendent streets of Sulaymaniyah, starting from Goizha to Hawara Barza, Tuy Melik, and Piramerd Street, his eyes are drawn to the majestic minarets and architectural wonders that adorn the cityscape. Each slender sentinel reaching towards heaven's minarets, old houses, old shops, and new architectural buildings stands as a testament to the historical grandeur and spiritual legacy of this remarkable city. For a moment he forgets all about Avan and stares at the streets and buildings.

He walks as he sees the buildings, with their intricate facades and ornate embellishments, exuding an aura of timeless elegance. They bear witness to the hands of craftsmen who painstakingly carved their mark upon the stone, etching a narrative of architectural brilliance that withstands the tests of time.

He inhales and exhales like a tired old man leaning on his cosy wooden walking stick as the city itself breathes with the echoes of civilizations past as if the very streets carry the weight of historical epochs. With every step, Aaron walks amidst a living tapestry woven by the hands of countless generations, where the ancient and the modern seamlessly intertwine until he reaches Sara Square. Sara Square teems with life, as vibrant markets and bustling bazaars unfold like theatrical stages. On one side, people are selling goldfish in small glass aquariums on the street and the opposite side, others are selling books. The aromas of tea, exotic sweets and baklava, and freshly baked naan bread fill the air, enticing the senses and beckoning wanderers to explore the treasures hidden within the labyrinthine alleys.

Amidst this architectural symphony, Aaron marvels at the harmonious blend of cultures and influences that shape Sulaymaniyah's identity. The Sara Building, the city statue, Mahmood Hafid, the founder of Sulaymaniyah Ibrahim Pasha Baban, Sir Oula sis, and Fayaq Bekas themselves bear witness to the city's storied past, reflecting the imprint of diverse civilizations that leave their mark upon its walls.

It is raining and a fresh breeze hits Aaron while he is still walking amidst the living testament to his city's rich historical buildings. The minarets and buildings stand as guardians of the city's collective memory, beckoning travellers to immerse themselves in the beauty and grandeur that emanate from every stone and structure. With each step, Aaron bears witness to the vibrant spirit of Kurdistan, a region that wears its history with pride and invites all who wander its streets: poets, writers, leaders, history, culture, buildings, and historical places to partake in its timeless allure. He puts his hand behind his back and walks fearlessly and carefree until he reaches the city centre. He arrived at the Great Mosque of Sulaimani, the mosque which was built by Ibrahim Pasha Baban in 1785. He waits in front of the Gate of the mosque and stares at the minaret and the pigeons in the sahn, courtyard, of the mosque.

He enters the mosque situated at the heart of the city which contains three cemeteries and the shrine of Haji Kaka Ahmed and his grandson, King Mahmood. Inside the Great Mosque of Sulaimani, a sense of awe washes over him, enveloping him in the sacred atmosphere that permeates the hallowed halls. The mosque, a masterpiece of architectural splendour, stands as a testament to the devotion and artistic ingenuity of those who constructed it.

The grandeur of the mosque unfolds before Aaron's eyes, as he beholds the soaring arches and intricately carved pillars that stretch towards the heavens. Each delicate detail tells a story, whispering of the skilled craftsmen who toil to bring this sanctuary to life, imbuing it with timeless elegance.

Sunlight, among the magic of swirling silver and grey clouds, streams through the stained glass windows, casting a mirage of hues upon the marble floors. As Aaron walks on this sacred ground, he feels the presence of history echoing throughout the chambers, where the footsteps of countless worshippers and scholars resonate throughout the ages.

The mihrab, a masterpiece of geometric patterns and calligraphic artistry, draws Aaron's gaze. Its intricate design serves as a focal point, directing the faithful towards Mecca, a symbolic bridge between the mortal realm and the divine. It is a testament to the unwavering devotion of those seeking solace and enlightenment within these sacred walls. Aaron directly starts his prayers deep inside himself between his soul and the Creator.

The rhythmic recitation of Quranic verses echoes softly in his ears, as worshippers find solace in their devotion. The ethereal sound, imbued with centuries of tradition, creates a mesmerising harmony that transcends time itself. The enduring power of faith and the spiritual legacy nurtured within these sacred confines is visible.

As Aaron continues his exploration of the mosque, he discovers secluded corners adorned with intricate mosaics depicting scenes from religious and historical narratives. The delicate tiles, painstakingly arranged, portray stories of mullahs, talibs, scholars, and noble figures who shape the course of humanity, a visual symphony that pays homage to the rich tapestry of human experience.

Now Aaron finds himself immersed in the splendour of the Great Mosque of Sulaimani. Its architectural magnificence and spiritual significance create an atmosphere of tranquillity and reverence. As he leaves the mosque from the back door, he carries with him a sense of gratitude for witnessing such a masterpiece, where the grandeur of the past and the devotion of the present coalesce into a profound experience of sacred beauty.

He heads to Mawlawi Street and the Public Park of Sulaimani. He passes by all those refreshments and pastries that fill his nose with the smell of fresh fruits and baklava. He walks down looking at people wearing thick clothes under their umbrellas. Aaron embarks on his stroll down Mawlawi Street, a thoroughfare steeped in the tapestry of time, the rainy winter season enveloping the city in a hushed symphony of droplets, casting a glistening veil upon the shops and street. The air is crisp, laden with the invigorating scent of petrichor, as people adorned in thick garments traverse the streets, seeking refuge from the chill in the embrace of warm fabrics.

As he navigates the wet cobblestones, his gaze drifts toward the Public Park of Sulaimani, nestled amidst the urban expanse. The park, a sanctuary of tranquillity, beckons him with its verdant allure, inviting respite from the bustling city rhythm. Along the way, he encounters friends, their figures cocooned in layers of wool and tweed.

Their greetings resound like harmonies, interweaving with the melody of raindrops, as they share anecdotes and laughter, a testament to the enduring bonds that withstand the test of seasons. Each encounter becomes a vignette, a tableau vivant in the ongoing saga of their parallel lives.

Aaron stops in a small café to grab an Americano. *Hello sir, Happy rainy day, can I have an Americano, please? No sugar, no milk. And please, for take away...* Aaron says. After he is served, he then walks along the road passing by the Post Office. He sees the park opposite the street and approaches it, finding solace beneath the leafy canopy of ancient trees, their branches embracing the raindrops like liquid jewels. The park, a haven for contemplation, provides a refuge from the bustling cityscape, as nature's gentle orchestra of rain and rustling leaves serenades his soul.

The park-goers, wrapped in heavy coats and scarves, form a tableau of resilience against the elements. Their presence echoes the collective spirit of generations past, who brave the harsh winters and find solace in the simple pleasures offered by nature. He sees couples walking hand in hand freely, an old man leaning on his stick walking around the park, a mom and her son chasing one another, a girl putting her book on her head to keep her hair from the rain droplets walking through the alley of the park.

As Aaron traverses the rain-soaked alleys of the park, he meets his friend, Rebwar, and he becomes a part of the living narrative of Sulaymaniyah. The city's history weaves through their conversations, mingling with the rhythm of rainfall, as they navigate the currents of time together. They talk about their university and work life. Aaron tells him about his current job as a Maths teacher in a school. Also, he tells Rebwar about his selected hobbies which are guitar playing and photography. He says *...I am not a professional, but a good guitarist and I am a professional photographer as I take pictures of marriage ceremonies and birthday parties from time to time.*

As the rain continues its gentle descent, Aaron and his friend revel in the camaraderie that the winter season brings, finding warmth not only in their snug attire but also in the enduring bonds of friendship. The rain-laden journey down Salim Street culminates in the peaceful sanctuary of the Public Park, where their collective presence echoes the resilience and unwavering spirit of the people who call this city home throughout history.

Aaron farewells Rebwar and heads toward the taxi station. He hails a yellow Corolla taxi. The taxi driver stops in front of him, and he hops in the taxi to go back to his cold and lonely apartment. He looks out of the window and looks at the city's streets and buildings while he is sitting in the front passenger seat of the taxi and drinks the last drops of his Americano...

Chapter Three

<u>O'Hare International Airport</u>

As Avan's mind swirled with the depth of her feelings for Aaron, much like the swirls of frothed milk on top of cappuccinos, the clock and time marched on. O'Hare International Airport is the size of an amusement park, like a department store with only two floors. The corridors and gates branch off like the veins on a maple leaf. There is an overall grandeur of this particular airport: with its waxy floors, international flights, and appearance in the classic movie *Home Alone.* Moms pushing strollers with tired toddlers, businessmen in peacoats carrying customised leather briefcases, big, wild families, students in oversized sweatshirts, athletes, and people wearing neck pillows crowded the distance between the petite, cramped corner Avan was currently sipping coffee in and her gate: C17. There was a lively tone to the airport, even at this hour. The preface of Christmas break, the chattering, the buzzing excitement of being soon reunited with loved ones. It made one temporarily forget about the stale air, filling one's nostrils with doom. Avan shifted in her chair to put on her charcoal grey tailored light blazer, careful not to muss up her hair. Avan did not want to attract attention to herself, but people tended to notice how put together she was. Even in a crowd, regrettably, she could never blend in. She enjoyed every minute of her respite spent plunged in a sea of nostalgia. Her heart was not as fortified as she remembered, not as carefree as in her youth. *The arrogance of youth will make you brave,* Avan thought. As people, we are meant for each other, and there is nothing we can do about it. We are not alone in this world, no matter how hard we might try to convince ourselves otherwise.

Pete's Coffee Shop was a bit of a distance from her gate. Avan had to navigate tables shoved together, families sprawled out, and the hullabaloo of holiday foot traffic. The overhead fluorescent lights were like spotlights illuminating the airport setting as if it was a theatrical stage premiering a Shakespeare play. Her Italian shoes take measured steps down the hallway. Gigantic red bows wrap around the gates, and shimmering, silver tinsel decorates the ceiling. Flight attendants and even pilots are wearing Christmas bows and ugly holiday sweaters. Avan's muted wardrobe, as she expects, provokes a series of looks from handsome men and curious children. Something about her expression, soft and mesmerised in thought, shines in profoundly romantic undercurrents. Even if she would never admit it.

Avan arrives at her gate, C17 where she sees clusters of people surrounding the entryway who are visibly miffed and exasperated. She glances from the big windows to the board saying "Flight 0927 delayed two hours due to stormy weather" and back at the window visibly displaying a malicious, tantrum of a snowstorm that looks like it is just beginning. There are a few people queued up with a recalcitrant glare in their eyes, starving for more information from the poor flight attendant behind the counter. Avan sighs. She finds a seat and plumps down, unzipping her canvas backpack and pulling out a book. She tries to read but a baby is crying a few feet away. People next to her are calling their relatives and explaining that their flight is delayed two hours. Luckily, this is the first leg of her trip, so she does not have to modify any pick-ups or arrangements. This is merely a hiccup. Things happen, that is life. Avan leans back in her chair for a moment and ponders.

As if she was in slow motion, and as if she was perched above a Norwegian fjord, Avan reaches into her jacket and pulls out her phone to call Aaron. Her heart is skipping jump rope in her chest, the blood coursing through her veins, and she suddenly has goosebumps, like she was on a cliff. Avan rarely is caught off guard, but this time, her manicured nails are repetitively tapping her right leg in anticipation. She is waiting with bated breath, simultaneously wanting Aaron to pick up but having absolutely no plan for what she would say if he does pick up his phone this time. *Can other people tell that I am pouncing out of my skin?* Avan wonders. A baby's toy rattle and jingle a few feet away, and yet again a lipsticked Southwest Airlines employee in a navy blue skirt and matching top comes on the intercom. *I am so sorry for the delay, everyone. We are working to defrost your aircraft as fast as we can. Then, we can begin the boarding process. Chicago is expecting 2-4 inches of snow and it is not safe to take off when the runway is icy. We will keep you posted. Come see me at the customer service desk with any questions. Merry Christmas, almost.* There is an ocean of chaos unfolding around her, but Avan is primarily concerned with quieting her clamouring heart. Aaron's phone rings once; Avan's heart bursts. It rings again. A tall, moustached man carrying onion rings from Arby's comes and sits directly next to Avan as the phone rings one more time. Aaron answers, and his voice is as velvety smooth as an ancient, chiselled Greek marble sculpture. Avan's voice sounds like a pair of wings that just carried themselves far away, to a mythical island.

"Avan, is that you?" Aaron musters.

"Hello, Aaron. Long time."

"Long time indeed."

There is a long pause before either of them speaks again, but they are fine in this strangely comforting silence. It is as if the years that have passed have instantly washed away from them, and even though they are on opposite sides of the world, they feel like they are standing opposite to each other, on the shore of a beach at dusk, the Barbie pink sun dissipating into the impressionistic, bubbly horizon. Avan's shaky hands and fear are immensely comforted just by hearing Aaron's voice. Everything is going to be okay. Avan is soothed by the subtext of their echoing and valley of silence. Her expression is beaming like moonlight. Her composure and poise are immediately melted like an ice cream cone melts in the summer. The people around her notice and smile, but do not say anything. Avan is momentarily eclipsed by the complex feelings in her chest. She needs to get some water. When she returns, still holding her mobile phone between her ear and her shoulder, she sees the board of her flight gate. Her flight is cancelled, only 45 minutes before it is supposed to take off. This information does not even register with Avan immediately. She settles into her seat.

"So, Aaron, are you free right now?"

"For you, I have all the time in the world."

"So do I, it seems, because (sighs) my flight has just been cancelled."

"Oh no! I am sorry to hear that."

"Yeah, me too. But I am also not. Because right now the only thing

that matters to me is the time I have at this moment on the phone with you, and somehow trying to find a way to bottle up how I feel right now so it can last longer than this phone call will. Even after all these years, look at what effect you have had on me. I know this sounds crazy-"

"Flight? Where are you headed?"

Avan begins to pour out her heart into this conversation, and Aaron, on the other line, listens intently, with wit and humour, both of which have withstood the test of the time they spent apart. She tells him about her future trip, her career, her cat, her car, her family, her life in the big city of Chicago, the city of big shoulders, the 3rd biggest city in America, and how lonely but awesome but wild her life is there. How she is going to get away for a bit and explore Italy. How she is single and watching her baby cousin get married. With each minute that passes, Avan becomes more bright on the line with her old, cherished, dear friend Aaron. The people that are sitting on either side of Avan smile knowingly. She looks fresh as a daisy, in the golden glow of love.

Avan settles into her airport seating, and her mind preoccupied with the imminent flight and the unforeseen turn of events. The resonating announcement echoes through the terminal, conveying the unfortunate cancellation of her flight due to the merciless snow and stormy weather outside.

The phone call with Aaron ends abruptly, leaving her with unanswered questions. She does not know whether it is from her side or his. *Is it due to the weather or does he have no service now?* Avan asks herself. As the unsettling news about the cancelled flight sinks in, memories of her dear sweet friend Aaron surge to the front of her mind, intertwining with the present moment like ivy climbing up a fence. She starts to imagine and create new stories about him and their relationship. She jumps to think of the what ifs: what if they shared a romantic friendship that bloomed amidst the enchanting allure of their youth? Avan's heart flutters as she delves into the recesses of her mind, back to the days when laughter and affection filled their lives. Their connection is unique, transcending the boundaries of conventional friendships. Like two souls dancing harmoniously, they used to explore the world with wide-eyed curiosity, cherishing each shared moment. They climbed mountains of joy and navigated valleys of sorrow, holding onto their bond, steadfast and unwavering. One particular winter, they found themselves in a magical snowstorm, when the world transformed into a mesmerising wonderland. Hand in hand, they twirled in the falling snowflakes, their laughter echoing through the crisp air. The warmth of their affection thawed the coldest of nights, creating a haven of love amidst the winter chill. But as time flowed onward, their lives led them on divergent paths, drawing them apart. Avan pursued her dreams in a distant city, while Aaron pursued his aspirations in a realm far from her reach. Yet, they remained deeply connected, their hearts entwined, regardless of the physical distance.

Now, as the airport announces the disruption of her plans, Avan finds solace in the past. She recalls the embrace of their romantic friendship, a love that knows no bounds, and her heart swells with a bittersweet blend of nostalgia and longing. The snow and stormy weather outside may interrupt her journey, but within her soul, the echoes of their friendship remain resilient and ever-present. With hope in her heart and memories as her guiding light, Avan knows that their love endures, transcending time and distance, forever embedded in the threads of their shared history.

Avan sits patiently in the airport, her eyes fixed on the departure board. Her flight is cancelled due to unforeseen circumstances, and she waits for any chance to catch another one. She decides to stroll around the gate area, observing the busy travellers and the airport's busy setting.

As she walks, she glances out the large windows at the runway, watching planes taxiing and taking off into the sky, but not her flight. The sight of the aircraft brings a sense of wonder and excitement, reminding her of the adventures that await her at her destination.

Inside the terminal, she observes a mother comforting her restless child, gently soothing their fears of not travelling and meeting their loved ones. Avan smiles at the heartwarming scene, remembering the care and love that parents provide in times of uncertainty.

She turns her attention to a group of friends reuniting, feeling a twinge of nostalgia. Their laughter and embraces speak of cherished memories and the joy of being together once again. Avan finds herself reminiscing about her own reunions with loved ones and the happiness those moments brought.

Among the crowd, she notices a group of students excitedly discussing their upcoming trip. Their backpacks and carry-on bags are filled with anticipation and adventure. Avan remembers the thrill of travelling during her student days, and a sense of camaraderie washes over her as she shares their excitement.

As the airport bustles around her, Avan finds solace in observing the diverse stories unfolding in every corner. Each person has their own journey, their own reasons for travel, and their own tales to tell.

Though her own flight is yet to be determined, Avan feels a newfound sense of peace. Amidst the uncertainties, she finds beauty in the simple act of observing and connecting with those around her. The airport becomes more than a waiting area; it becomes a place of shared moments and unspoken connections, a reminder that, in the vast world of travel, we are all intertwined in our journeys. It is a miracle she and Aaron met. There are millions of people in the world, and she was lucky enough to cross paths with him.

After her flight faces that unfortunate cancellation, she decides to make the most of her time at the airport by heading to the alluring realm of the duty-free shops. She meanders through the concourse, her eyes captivated by the array of enticing boutiques and shops adorned with a rich assortment of souvenirs and treasures from around the world.

With an air of anticipation, Avan peruses the delightful display of souvenirs, each item promising to encapsulate the essence of her travels and evoke cherished memories. Her discerning eye seeks out the finest keepsakes, those imbued with cultural richness and artistic craftsmanship.

Her fingers delicately trace the intricacies of handcrafted trinkets, each one a testament to the skilful hands that bring them to life. Vibrant textiles adorned with indigenous patterns whisper tales of ancient traditions, while exquisite jewellery sparkles like stardust, capturing the allure of distant lands.

Avan's mind dances as she contemplates the significance of each purchase, considering the sentiments they will hold for her and her loved ones at home or abroad. She is not sure whether to buy anything for Aaron or not, as she is not quite sure whether she will meet him again one day or not. She still has the birthday gifts she bought him years ago, never getting an exact mailing address from him to send them to. With every acquisition, she aims to transport a piece of the world's wonders to his doorstep, a tangible reminder of the adventure that has eluded her for the moment. However, she still does not know his home, work, or even office address, as he always says that they do not have P.O. Boxes or mailing addresses. *What a country!* She thinks.

In the sanctuary of the duty-free haven, time seems to blur, as if the confines of the airport's walls are replaced with the magic of a global night market. The vibrant tapestry of cultures unfurls before her, and Avan immerses herself in this exquisite realm, traversing borders in pursuit of precious tokens of her travels.

Ultimately, as she emerges from the treasure trove of souvenirs, Avan carries with her a treasure trove of memories and aspirations. Despite the flight cancellation, her spirits remain lifted, for she knows that the world's wonders are ever within her grasp, and her heart brims with the anticipation of future journeys yet to be embarked upon.

She could not buy anything in the duty-free shop since her heart needs something way beyond that, way beyond material stuff, or at least fresh air and a coffee outside somewhere away from all the humans. She decides to head to the ticket counter inside the airport, determined to find an alternative plan for her disrupted travel. Her flight is cancelled, leaving her eager to salvage her Christmas break and holiday. As she approaches the counter, she takes a deep breath, preparing to engage with the ticket counter clerk in a warm and friendly manner.

With a smile on her face, Avan explains her predicament to the clerk, expressing her disappointment about the cancelled flight. She shares her desire for a new ticket to a destination somewhere close to and by a serene lake. Her eyes shimmer with hope as she envisions a peaceful getaway amidst nature's tranquillity.

The ticket counter employee appreciates Avan's friendly approach and listens attentively to her request. She sees her genuine enthusiasm and understands the inconvenience caused by the flight cancellation, eager to assist her in finding a suitable solution.

After some friendly banter and exchanging holiday wishes, she gives Avan a couple of options for destinations nearby with beautiful lake houses. She discusses the available flights and amenities, ensuring that Avan's Christmas break will be relaxing.

As the conversation continues, Avan and the ticket counter clerk forge a positive connection, sharing stories and laughter. The clerk empathises with Avan's desire for a memorable holiday experience and is committed to making her journey as enjoyable as possible.

With the ticket issue resolved, Avan expresses her gratitude to the employee for their exceptional assistance. They part ways, but not before exchanging warm smiles and well wishes for the holiday season.

Avan heads towards her new destination, feeling grateful for the unexpected turn of events that led her to a delightful lake house retreat. Along the way, she reflects on the power of friendly communication and how a positive approach can create meaningful connections with others, even amidst travel challenges.

As she embarks on her Christmas break adventure, Avan knows that the holiday spirit is not confined to a specific destination. It is the genuine interactions and shared moments of kindness that make the season truly special. And so, with excitement in her heart, she looks forward to creating cherished memories by the lake, embraced by the warmth of newfound friendship and holiday cheer.

She heads toward her gate, a new gate, a new life, toward a new destination; just like life paths. She looks at her new ticket while she folds her old ticket and puts it into her pocket. *Look at this compensation; wow, such a stroke of luck!*

Flight cancellation! Now a free new ticket to a lake house as a Christmas gift. Hey, Santa, is that you? Avan murmurs. The new gate is A 12. She heads to A 12 to start her new journey by the lake...

Chapter Four

<u>The Moor Shack</u>

Aaron is on the other end of the line on the other end of the world when Avan stops biting her nails nervously and decides to call him. At that moment, Aaron is nestled a few hundred kilometres away from his home in Sulaymaniyah. In a tucked away moor shack, he is residing for a few days of serenity to put a spring back in his step again, as the saying goes. The moor shack is most similar to a cob house in the west, stunning in its own quiet way and made strong by hand, sturdy enough to withstand winter storms, heavy rain, or gusts of wind. They look like acrylic paintings someone spent a lot of time on during each season– summer, autumn, spring, and winter, Aaron's favourite.

They are places to go to think deeply and to feel even deeper without interruption. In exchange for a more spartan lifestyle, the moor shack and its environment go above and beyond for you: a crystal clear star party every night where stars are speckled across the magnificent darkened sky, a blood orange-red sunrise that shocks you like taking a sip of grapefruit juice. And everything in between. During the day, Aaron could see all the trees on the moor, their roots unwavering. The green pastures with their various shades of forest green, sage, emerald, and fern. It is a place that transcends time itself. It is both ancient and timeless, where Aaron's precious assumptions about the purity of nature are rescinded. Its beauty lies in the fact that after centuries, it remains untouched. Rain, wind, and snow cannot change it even slightly. The landscape goes on for what seems like forever. You cannot help but marvel at it.

It is a structure whence you can see the gorgeous moon on display, smell the fresh mountain air, watch a blanket of pristine snow gather atop the bristled branches of trees and hear the occasional chirps of migratory birds in 'V' formations. You could sit all day and watch the birds here, like you are in Greece, gazing at them, jealous of their flight.

It is a simple getaway, a writer's retreat. Since moor shacks are old, they require more time, attention, upkeep, and care than most city people are accustomed to. But Aaron does not mind. Not that the work associated with where you live or stay is menial by any means. In fact, it is the opposite. Heating the moor shack, starting a fire, shovelling snow, cleaning the window panes, keeping dirt out, it is all a delicate art. Preserving structures as old as the mountains is a way of keeping history alive. It is out of respect, an appreciation for tradition, and a symbolic defiance of modern society that tells us we need to buy this and that to be happy. Only when you travel to a moor shack or anywhere along the coast of nature do you realise that as humans we must protect nature at all costs because nature gives us oxygen, soil to grow plants and food, water, grass, trees, the sun, the moon, the stars, the mountains? It makes us feel alive and happy. It gives us life. So what more, really, can we ask for?

In fact, Aaron relishes the opportunity for solitude and a few days to explore the moor and let his thoughts slowly drift. Fluffy white clouds pass like ephemeral dancing shadows playing tricks with light. The moor shack seamlessly blends in with its natural surroundings like a chameleon. It is not an easy place to stay, but it is worth it for the ever-expanding views of the sunrise, and the fully immersive experience of being able to see all the stars visibly. Sometimes he can even see Venus and Mars and, if Aaron is lucky, a shooting star. The moor shack is on a steep incline, it faces east so the sun floods the structure in the early mornings, warming him up a little even on the coldest, most crisp winter day.

It is somewhere he keeps coming back to. There is no place like it. This is the last thought that filters through his mind before he retreats to a slumber that almost feels intoxicating. After his final month of teaching before Christmas break, with all the scrambling, red marker, grading, teaching, and endless cups of coffee, he has been sleeping so well.

Avan calls him in the middle of the night. She regrets waking him up but does not see that in her present minor calamity, she has much of a choice. Aaron is calm until his mobile phone rings. Though after not talking much to anyone the past couple of days– not his students, their parents, his neighbours, local shopkeepers, or even his friends, he decides to pick up his phone. He does not want to miss another one of Avan's calls. He has the birds that usually wake him up to talk to if he so wishes. How long has it been again since they last spoke? Aaron wonders. How many years? How strange it is because they used to be inseparable. They used to talk every single day, as much as they could fit into their busy student schedules. Avan would look for Aaron's face first in a crowd. Like a moth goes to a flame, the two friends were brought together by cosmic forces above them both. Why, neither of them was ever certain. But Aaron always told Avan not to question it, and that friendship is better because it lasts longer. It broke Avan's heart because all she ever did was love him, against her better judgement. Against logic and reason, despite their difference in background, culture, and language, she loved him with every cell and molecule in her body, and it was enough to make her tremble.

"Avan, is that you?" Aaron musters.

Aaron gets up to get a glass of water. He clumsily walks into the pitch-black kitchen, narrowly avoiding the furniture, forgetting entirely that the moor shack does not have any street lights surrounding it to guide him. Only the moonbeams and sparkling stars that simultaneously seem close and far away could have lit the way.

"Hello, Aaron. Long time." Avan, her voice is still like milk and honey.

There was a pause. Aaron took a sip of water, set it down, and peered out of the kitchen window into the peaceful winter landscape that he knew could make people cold to the bone.

"Long time indeed," Aaron says coyly. In his pyjamas and tank top, he forces himself to be alert for this conversation. He puts his phone down to splash some water on his face and even cracks the front door to get a blast of cold air. Aaron is glad he did. Avan still gushes when she talks to him, which Aaron finds adorable but would never dare admit to her face. Avan's words are gushing out. She is at the airport, and he can hear muffled conversations and a cacophony of noises as the backdrop to her overflowing words. She sounds a bit distraught, she tells him her flight was cancelled. She is on a break as well, and now, instead of going to Italy a few days early, she is going to a lakehouse in Lake Geneva, Wisconsin, for a few days until the weather settles down and the snowstorm passes. Aaron listens intently, chiming in when necessary, soothing her worries. It is as if no time has passed between them. In the quietness of the moor shack, Avan's words, the subtext behind them, and her true feelings are outstretched, tended to and mended by Aaron. Aaron tells her about his trip to Egypt. At that point, he hesitates. He wonders if she would want to meet up with him in Egypt before the Italy trip. Is that crazy? He thinks it does not hurt to ask her. So he proposes the plan, leaning against the kitchen door frame and waiting for her response.

It was such a lazy day for both Aaron and Avan. Avan is in the airport on the other side of the world on the phone with Aaron in a shack, with the sun casting a warm glow through the window while snow can still be found on the ground outside. Aaron and Avan find themselves engaged in a heartfelt phone conversation that traverses the realms of their shared past, the tapestry of their friendship, and the countless escapades they have embarked upon together.

With a smile in his voice, Aaron begins, "Hey Avan, do you remember that time we decided to be spontaneous and took that impromptu road trip? The car we hired from that rental car company? The car broke down in the middle of nowhere, and we had to channel our inner MacGyver to get back on the road?"

Avan's voice fills with heartily laughter and nostalgia on the other end of the line. "Oh man, that was a classic! We turned into amateur mechanics with our makeshift tools. We kept repeating a 'when life gives you lemons' moment, right?"

Their laughter fills the airwaves, bridging the distance between them. Avan then brings up their hiking expedition to that mystical forest. "And let's not forget that time we hiked to that hidden waterfall. We got lost in the wilderness and stumbled upon that charming clearing. It was like a scene straight out of a fairytale."

Aaron's voice is tinged with amusement. "Absolutely! We were like explorers in a storybook, stumbling upon secret realms. The mud-splattered clothes and tangled hair were all worth it for that breathtaking view."

Their reminiscing leads them down memory lane, as Aaron recounts their late-night conversations during their travels. "You know, those late drives beneath the starlit sky were the perfect backdrop for our deep talks. It was like our personal 'philosophy under the moon' sessions."

Avan's voice holds an iota of nostalgia. "Oh, I cherished those moments. We discussed life, dreams, and the mysteries of the universe, all while the world slept around us. It was like the road became our confessional."

The timbre of their conversation shifts and Avan playfully remarks, "And let's not overlook our daring culinary adventures. That time we dared to conquer the 'spiciest dish in town' challenge? I still get heartburn just thinking about it!"

Aaron's laughter echoes through the phone. "Oh goodness, I had never seen you turn that shade of red before! We thought we could handle the heat, but that dish was like a fire-breathing dragon."

As the minutes tick by, their stories continue to flow, painting a vivid picture of their unbreakable bond. Avan then shares, "You know, no matter where we went or what we did, our friendship was our compass. Through highs and lows, we were each other's constants."

Aaron's voice softens. "Absolutely, Avan. Our adventures were the backdrop, but our friendship was the heart of it all. From the thrilling to the mundane, you were my partner in crime."

And so, across the thousands of miles and kilometres, their conversation weaves a tapestry of shared memories and cherished moments. As the sun shines across the mountains and tree leaves, their connection remains strong, a testament to the enduring friendship that Aaron and Avan nurtured all those years ago. After their trip down memory lane, Aaron reluctantly hangs up the call, leaving Avan to finish her tasks in the bustling airport. He assures her that he will go out for a walk to explore the surroundings near his shack. With a promise to catch up later, they exchange a fond farewell, their connection lingering even after the call ends. As he steps out into the unfamiliar landscape, Aaron's excitement to discover the hidden gems around his temporary abode grows, eager to create new memories in a place that is yet to be explored. *It is snowing and the sun shines at the same time, what a coincidence* he thinks.

It is almost late afternoon, and as the sun begins its descent, Aaron feels the call of the moor near his humble shack. Bundled up in his cosy attire, he steps out with an eagerness to immerse himself in the untamed beauty that surrounds him. The moor stretches out before him like a vast, tranquil canvas painted in shades of muted greens and serene browns, its ruggedness a testament to nature's unbridled artistry.

With each step, the crunch of frost beneath his boots sings a melody of the season. The brisk air nips at his cheeks, invigorating his senses with the crispness that only winter can provide. He is on a journey, not just through the moor, but through his own thoughts and reflections, accompanied by the distant symphony of rustling leaves and the occasional caw of a solitary crow.

As Aaron wanders deeper into the heart of the moor, he finds himself amid a delicate dance between light and shadow. The slanting rays of the sun transform the landscape into a breathtaking tableau, casting long, enigmatic silhouettes that seem to tell stories of forgotten ages. He feels like an explorer, unearthing secrets that lay hidden within the folds of time.

Stumbling upon a gnarled tree standing like a guardian of the moor, Aaron cannot resist the urge to rest against its sturdy trunk. With a contented sigh, he allows himself to become one with nature, his thoughts flowing like the rivulets that are like a maze throughout the landscape. In the distance, the silvery waters of a brook reflect the waning sunlight, a serene reminder of the interconnectedness of all living things.

As the sky morphs into hues of rose and amber, Aaron cannot help but marvel at the transient beauty of the moment. He is a mere spectator in nature's grand theatre, where the stars above and the earth below choreograph a symphony of stillness. In this serene haven, time feels as though it has momentarily halted, allowing him to savour the present without the burden of the past or the demands of the future.

As Twilight paints the moor in shades of indigo and lavender, Aaron reluctantly begins his journey back to his shack. Each step feels like a bittersweet farewell to the realm of nature's embrace. Yet, he carries with him a sense of renewal, a rekindled connection with the world around him. In the silence of the late afternoon, Aaron has found solace and rediscovered the art of simply being, a gift that nature has generously offered to him in the heart of winter.

Nestled within his moor shack, Aaron finds himself in the middle of a winter's night sitting inside the shack, a scene that seems to belong to the pages of a classic novel. Before him, the samovar crackles and radiates its gentle warmth, casting a comforting glow that dances on the walls. The aroma of steaming chamomile tea fills the air, a fragrant invitation to relax. The world outside may be wrapped in a snowy embrace, but within the walls of his haven, a world of solace awaits.

With a contented sigh, Aaron cradles the teacup in his hands, feeling the heat seep into his fingertips, thawing the chill of the evening. The steam spirals upward like a wisp of magic, carrying with it the aroma of the herbs that promise calmness and serenity. He takes a slow, deliberate sip, savouring the moment as if time itself has decided to linger awhile.

Beside the steaming cup, his favourite book rests, its pages inviting him to delve into a different world. He runs his fingers over the well-worn cover, a tangible connection to stories that keep him company through many nights. The words within hold the power to transport him to distant lands, to kindle the fires of imagination that burn brighter than any winter star.

As the night deepens, the moon casts its silver sheen through the white clouds and the frost-kissed window, painting the room in a soft, ethereal glow. Aaron's attention shifts from the tea to the book, his eyes tracing the lines that breathe life into characters and tales. He is not just reading, he is embarking on a journey, wandering through the intricate paths of literature that wind their way through his thoughts.

In the murmur of the winter night, Aaron loses track of time, completely immersed in the world he holds in his hands. Outside, the winds may whisper secrets to the trees, and the stars may engage in their celestial dance, but within his moor shack, he is forging a connection with the author whose words are in his hands.

As the last pages are turned and the final sips of tea are taken, Aaron sets his book aside. He gazes into the depths of the grey metal wood stove, the flames dancing like the flickering memories of a distant past. The night weaves its enchantment around him, leaving him grateful for the warmth of his haven and the escape that literature provides. He goes out to bring more logs and puts them aside the wood stove to make sure that he has enough logs until morning and he will not have to go out in the middle of the night to bring in more firewood.

With a satisfied smile, Aaron leans back, his heart and mind nourished by the dual magic of tea and prose. In his moor shack, with the winter's embrace outside and the comfort within, he realises that this moment is a treasure worth cherishing, a sanctuary where the world outside can wait a little longer, and the stories within can unfold like a red carpet.

Reclining on a finely woven Kurdish rug, Aaron finds himself in a moment of introspection, his hand tracing the intricate patterns as if deciphering the mystique of his own past. Under him, a plush Kurdish pillow cradles his head, offering comfort and support as he gazes into the dancing flames of the samovar and wood stove. The room is a haven of warmth and nostalgia, a space where the present meshes with memories of his youth, particularly his vibrant college days. Just beside the stove, a tray can be found which has a teacup, a saucer, and some homemade sugar cubes in a small wooden bowl on it.

As his thoughts wander through the corridors of time, Aaron's mind becomes a gallery of recollections, each memory a brushstroke on the canvas of his life. He recalls the days when the world seems boundless, his aspirations as grand as the dreams that danced in his eyes. The days of youthful exuberance, where challenges are met with a grin and hurdles are merely stepping stones.

The samovar's steam spirals upward, mirroring the tendrils of thoughts that curl through his mind. Proverbs he hears from elders come to life, reminding him that "youth is the time of getting, middle age of improving, and old age of spending." Indeed, he muses, life's seasons carry wisdom within them, and he has embraced the lessons each phase brings.

The crackling of the wood stove, akin to the rhythm of life's journey, transports Aaron back to his college years. The nights of burning the midnight oil, fueled by ambition and camaraderie, come alive like vivid scenes from a movie.

He can almost hear the bursts of laughter, the passionate debates in lecture halls, and the shared stories over late-night snacks.

The Kurdish pillow under his head cradles not just comfort, but the nostalgia of youthful friendships, where bonds are forged amidst trials and triumphs. He remembers a Kurdish proverb that says, "A friend is known in adversity like gold is known in a fire." Those are the fires that form his friendships, creating unbreakable ties.

As Aaron lies there, the room transforms into a sanctuary of reflection. The samovar and wood stove become vessels of memory, and the Kurdish rug and pillow, witnesses to his journey. The tea cup and sugar cubes remind him of old gatherings with his grandparents. With a sigh that carries both wistfulness and contentment, he embraces the truth of the saying, "Youth comes but once in a lifetime, cherish it."

In this moment of contemplation, Aaron understands that while the years have added layers to his experiences, the core of his youthful spirit remains intact. With a smile, he gazes at the patterns on the rug, each thread a reminder of his intricate story. The samovar's soft hum and the wood stove's crackle become the soundtrack of his memories, a serenade to his journey from young aspirations to the seasoned wisdom he holds today.

After a peaceful slumber that night, Aaron awakens to the soft morning light filtering through the curtains of his moor shack. Stretching leisurely, he rises from his bed and prepares to greet the new day. With a sense of purpose, he dons his cosy attire and sets about preparing a hearty breakfast. The sizzle of eggs in the skillet and the aroma of fresh coffee fill the air, promising a delicious start to the day.

As Aaron sits down to enjoy his breakfast, he contemplates the day ahead. With the warmth of his meal energising him, he feels a renewed vigour to explore the area around him.

Stepping outside, Aaron is greeted by the crispness of the morning air. His footsteps mark a path through the snow-kissed leaves, as he sets out on his walk. Each step is a journey of curiosity, a chance to uncover hidden treasures amidst nature's splendour. The world around him seems to hum with life, and he is an eager participant in its production.

As the day rolls on, Aaron finds himself immersed in a rhythm of tranquillity. The art of preparing dishes and cooking for himself becomes more than just sustenance; it is a celebration of self-reliance and the joy of creation. The old adage: "The way to a person's heart is through their stomach" takes on new meaning as he savours his culinary creations with a sense of accomplishment.

It is not just the kitchen that occupies his time. Aaron's wanderlust leads him to explore the rolling moors, the meandering paths, and the hidden pockets of beauty that nature has hidden into the landscape. Each step is a metaphor for embracing life's journey, for "Life is a journey that must be travelled no matter how bad the roads and accommodations."

Walking beneath the open sky, he finds himself immersed in the beauty of the present moment. The cares of the city seem like a distant memory as he absorbs the serenity around him. The quote: "In every walk with nature, one receives far more than he seeks" becomes his mantra, as the quietude of the natural world overflows his mind and soul.

As the week unfolds, Aaron's days are a mosaic of culinary experiments, solitary walks, and moments of quiet contemplation. The weeks are known to be the longest time, especially in the last week of the month, but time seems to slip by unnoticed in his refuge. His heart is light, his mind is refreshed, and his spirit is rejuvenated.

In this tranquil haven away from the hustle of the city, Aaron discovers that there is truth in the proverb "Nature does not hurry, yet everything is accomplished." He learns that sometimes, the most profound discoveries and transformations happen in the midst of stillness. And as he continues to immerse himself in the rhythm of his days, Aaron realises that life's most meaningful moments are often found in the simplest of joys...

Chapter Five

<u>The Lake House: Lake Geneva, Wisconsin</u>

"Look at this compensation; wow, such a stroke of luck! Flight cancellation! Now a free new ticket to a lake house in Lake Geneva, Wisconsin as a Christmas gift. Hey, Santa, is that you?" Avan recalls her final, playful thought before boarding her new flight yesterday. It is the only way truly to enjoy her break, Avan forces herself not to dwell on what went wrong. Sometimes, maybe, just maybe, it'll lead you to something better. Avan ponders. She is flummoxed. Wishful thinking.

It is early morning. There are large bay windows on each side of her room facing north, east, and west flooding her space with the light blue morning sunlight and a few puffs of clouds. The room she wakes up in at first unsettles her. So much had happened the day before and her surroundings were at first unfamiliar. The bedroom she is in is painted in a similar periwinkle colour with white trim, matching pastel pillows, a quilt, a white, wicker bedside table, and a lamp decorated with a mosaic of seashells. Her rolling suitcase is placed at the end of her bed on an old, metal, iron trunk, which seems anachronistic compared to the beachy vibe of the room. The wooden door to her bedroom, also painted white, with its old, crystal glass doorknob, is not fully closed. *Should I be alarmed?* Avan muses. *Or was I so exhausted from the day that I did not quite shut the door all the way?* Again she murmured.

Directly across from her queen-sized bed, there was a bay window with a stack of throw pillows on one side and a flower box with bright pink dahlias planted below the window frame on the other. Avan inhales. The air is fresh here, less polluted than a big, bustling city. It smells of lavender, laundry detergent, and very faintly of coffee. Avan sighs happily. Her Airbnb is quaint without being rustic. It is a charming, two-story cottage right near Lake Geneva. It is where you can lose track of time and relive a simpler lifestyle. The beachfront, Riviera Beach, is about a four-minute walk from the back porch of the cottage. It is big and blue and many residents walk with friends, walk their dogs, or bring their children or grandchildren in the winter, in lieu of swimming. She is torn between wanting to remain cosy in her big, quilted, comfortable bed, sinking into a memory foam pillow or going outside and strolling, to see the scenery. Avan opts to go out because why not, she only has a few days here, so she might as well explore. Her adventurous spirit wins again.

Let me see who is here in Lake Geneva at Christmas time, Avan decides. Lake Geneva, Wisconsin is a popular destination for Chicagoans to visit during the summer before the cicadas buzz and sing so loudly it drags out the end of summer, especially when the humidity is too much. Lake Geneva is a proper lake destination with lake houses. It is natural. Since it is winter, most of the trees are bare and Avan can spot a few red, orange, and yellow leaves, leftover from autumn, strewn about the frozen ground. Even though it is cold, there are still people milling about, smiling, and in mittened hands holding hot beverages that release plumes of smoke into the cold air.

It is a short flight and a few hours to drive here from Chicago. A stone arched wall wraps around the lake. Wisconsin is the cheese state, with very good craft beer and sausages as well. What is not to love? However, since it is north of Chicago, it is colder. Where Avan is staying is winterized, however. It is toasty in her room. She immediately puts on thick, wool socks. She dresses in layer after layer and heads down the creaky, hardwood floored hallway, down the old spiral stairs that more resemble a fire escape, and out the back door that dings a bell and wind chimes whenever someone enters or exits. Avan's glasses fog up as soon as she hits the cold air.

No one else at the Bed and Breakfast seems to be awake yet, or, if they are, they are already out foraging for breakfast. Avan hopes to see a Great Blue heron bird at the lake or a woodpecker. *How do all the birds know where to migrate, year after year?* Avan watches her thoughts float on like a duck floats on a lake, going with the flow of the water.

After pacing at the airport for many hours yesterday and trying to find a comfortable way to nap on the plane (this much she did learn– there is no way, you can only press your face against the teeny airport window, close your eyes, and hope you can sleep through any babies crying or obnoxious passengers asking for yet again another thing: a blanket, headphones, ginger ale, you name it...) she is ready for a long walk. This destination to Lake Geneva was totally unexpected, so she does not have an idea about how to spend her days here. It is time to get creative and do her best with what she has. The waves on the lake gently lap, and even though it is cold, it is peaceful, which, to Avan, is a worthy trade. Wisconsin is so big. There is so much to see here and beyond. Avan's winter boots (actually hiking boots) crunch fallen leaves and frost on the wintry ground. She decides to walk until her cheeks are too red and her teeth are too cold and until she cannot take it anymore, and then she will return to her room and plot her next move. There is nothing a cup of tea cannot fix. Or pizza for that matter. As Avan walks, she thanks whoever is up there that she was not on a dangerous aircraft in a winter snowstorm. Even though it is bitterly cold in Wisconsin and she has yet to come up with a concrete plan for this section of her trip, she is safe. She reaches into her puffy, teal winter coat and smiles, feeling a lighter and a packet of cigarettes. She must have left these in there from last year. It is an occasional habit, one that she enjoys immensely. Not a lot of people know that she smokes. The cigarette smoke mixes with the wind, steadying her nerves. Aaron knows she smokes. They used to sneak out after class and smoke, many moons ago. Avan smiles and wipes her nose on a handkerchief. It was her and Aaron against the world.

Avan finishes a big loop around Riviera Beach, looking for sea glass, seashells, and interesting-looking rocks along the way. [She collects rocks and has since she was 5 years old. One time, at her great-aunt Frances's beach house in Rhode Island, she filled an entire bucket with rocks and was extremely upset that her mother did not allow her to take the bucket with her when they were about to leave to return home. "You can pick one or two!" her mom told her. Aunt Frances watched the whole thing happen, and saw it coming from far away.] Although, on second thought, what was she going to do? Bring rocks with her in her suitcase? By the time she reaches the cottage, her cheeks are pink and her hands feel disconnected from her body. She leans against the front door to open it so she can avoid taking her mittens off. Her host, an older lady named Beatrice, greets her when she walks in.

"Marcus, is that you?" Beatrice calls out from the kitchen.

"No! This is Avan!" Avan says as she walks toward the cosy kitchen.

Beatrice is holding a tea kettle and filling it with water.

"Oh, sorry, I thought you were my husband. He has just popped out to get more firewood and some stevia sweetener. Not all of our guests take sugar in their coffee or tea, and I want to make sure everyone has a comfortable stay. Would you like some coffee?"

"Sure, I would love some." Avan smiles. The host of this cottage is like her grandmother, only more southern.

"You can put your scarf and mittens on this radiator to dry them, dear. Be careful though, it is hot." Beatrice points to a black radiator.

"Alright, thank you!" Avan unravels her scarf and lays it out on the hissing, hot radiator. Her voice is mellifluous, as if Beatrice's warmth has melted her worries.

"Cream or sugar?" Beatrice asks as she pours Avan a mug of coffee.

"Just cream, please, thanks."

Beatrice sets the coffee down on an old-timey, circular coaster with ducks on it in front of Avan.

"Did you sleep okay last night?" Beatrice chirps.

"Yes, thank you, I slept like a rock." Avan feels refreshed from her walk.

Even though she is severed from her original plan, this new place will do just fine. She can find fun anywhere.

"You just let me or Marcus know if you need anything, dear. You know, we do not get guests in the winter too often, but we are happy to have the company. It is usually quiet these days. Where are you coming from by the way?" Beatrice inquires.

"Oh, I just got in late last night from Chicago. Actually, my original flight was cancelled because of the snowstorms in the northeast, and the airline gave me a brand new, free ticket to Lake Geneva. So here I am." Avan explains, trying to obfuscate the tone of disappointment in her voice.

Beatrice tells Avan there is a small Christmas party in town this evening, with violinists, beer, and swing dancing. Avan amicably accepts the invitation, glad that she has something to do. Avan excuses herself, retreats to her bedroom, and calls Aaron. She is certain that Aaron will know what to say, and advise her on where to go from there. She does not mind Lake Geneva for a few days, but after that, it will become boring. At least right now, though, the views are novel, sparkling, they are spectacular. This touristy town is charming, nice, and expansive. A fleet of sailboats is near a dock to the left of her bedroom, and to her right, the beginning of the walking path, with a 3-foot high stone wall that continues around the perimeter of the lake. Avan is cosy, and at the moment, that is all that matters. Avan sings quietly to herself the song: *What a Wonderful World* by Louis Armstrong. Nature does not hurry, yet everything is accomplished. Avan suddenly feels that she will accomplish everything she set out for this winter break, including new experiences, adventure, and rest. She slows down, listening to her breathing, and takes out her phone.

Avan sits by the window, gazing out at the picturesque landscape that stretches as far as the eye can see. The Lake House in Lake Geneva, Wisconsin, is a dream come true. She can't resist sharing her enchanting experience with her close friend [or a lover, who knows; even they are both lost and left with no names], Aaron. Excitement bubbles within her as she dials his number.

As the phone rings, Avan taps her fingers lightly on the wooden table, awaiting Aaron's answer. Finally, he picks up, his voice a warm embrace through the line. "Hello, Avan! How's your stay at The Lake House?"

A delighted smile graces Avan's face as she begins to narrate her day. "Aaron, you won't believe the sheer beauty of this place. The Lake House is a haven tucked away from the bustling world, and I feel like I stepped into a postcard. The winter sun kisses the lake, painting it in a golden hue, and the trees look like something out of a fairytale." She talks to Aaron in a low but dramatic tone.

Aaron can almost visualise the scenery through Avan's vivid descriptions. "It sounds absolutely magical, Avan. Tell me more about your day." He asks Avan to continue as he realises he has missed her voice.

Avan continues, "Well, I started my morning with a brisk walk around the gardens, the crisp air invigorating my senses. After that, I retreated to the cosy small library on the corner of the street, where I curled up with a classic novel and sipped on some Mexican hot chocolate. Actually, it was served by the librarian as part of the place's tradition. It felt like a scene from a period drama, I swear. This would never happen in Chicago!" Again she reminds Aaron of the small, dusty bookstore they went to years ago. "Do you remember once upon a time we were so close that we chose books for each other and competed on who would finish the book first and win an invitation to MAAN's Café?" she adds to her previous speech.

Aaron chuckles, knowing how much Avan loves immersing herself in books. "And what is on the agenda for this evening?"

Avan's voice takes on a tone of anticipation as she replies, "The best part is yet to come, my dear friend [let's say that]. The gracious owner of The Lake House invited me to a small Christmas party tonight. The house is adorned with sparkling lights and wreaths, and the aroma of holiday treats waft through the air. It is going to be a soirée to remember." "Would you mind if I join them?" she adds.

Aaron grins on the other end of the line. "Avan, you're living the dream! Enjoy every moment of it, and don't forget to share all the juicy details of the party with me later."

Avan nods, her heart filled with gratitude for this once-in-a-lifetime experience. "I promise, Aaron. I feel truly lucky to be here, and I can't wait to soak in the holiday spirit tonight like a sea sponge. It's as if The Lake House comes alive and weaves its magic around me."

As the conversation draws to a close, Avan cannot help but feel that her stay at The Lake House is like a chapter from a fairy tale—a tale she will cherish and share with her dear friend Aaron for years to come.

After Avan ends her call with Aaron, she heads downstairs to catch up with Beatrice and meet up with Marcus. The anticipation of the upcoming Christmas party and her eagerness to explore the must-see places in Lake Geneva, Wisconsin fill her with excitement.

She finds Beatrice in the living room, a room decked out with plush velvet furniture and a crackling fireplace. Beatrice, an elegant and welcoming lady, greets Avan again with a warm smile and a twinkle in her eye. "Avan, dear, how did your call go? I heard you were on the phone. Sorry I do not mean to intrude, but it reminds me of my early days with Marcus." She chuckles.

Avan settles into a plush armchair and sighs with contentment. "Oh, Beatrice, it went wonderfully. Aaron, he is the one who I talked to, kind of friend, best friend, soul mate, lover; well we do not know yet, was over the moon to hear about my stay here at The Lake House. He can't wrap his head around the sheer beauty of this place, and to be honest, neither can I."

Beatrice chuckles softly, her laughter sounding like crinkling wrapping paper. "I'm thrilled that you're having a great time here, my dear. Now, let's discuss the Christmas party if you are here to talk about that or in case you would like to join. We have quite the evening planned. The grand hall shines with a thousand candles, and the smell of delicious treats fills the air, teasing your senses. It's a soirée that has been the talk of the town every year for years."

Avan's eyes light up with anticipation. "I can hardly wait, Beatrice. It sounds absolutely enchanting. Is there anything I should be aware of or prepare for?"

Beatrice leans in, speaking in hushed tones. "Well, we have a little tradition here at The Lake House. We encourage every guest to wear a festive sweater, and the wilder, the better. We're even having a competition for the most creative one. So, if you happen to have a quirky Christmas sweater hidden away in your closet or bag, now is the time to dig it out."

Avan grins, imagining herself in a whimsical Christmas sweater. "I'll make sure to find the quirkiest one I can."

As their conversation turns to the finer details of the Christmas party, Marcus, the friendly concierge of The Lake House, joins them. He is a treasure trove of information about the local area, and Avan cannot wait to hear his recommendations for must-see places.

Marcus greets Avan with a warm handshake. "Good afternoon, Avan. I heard you were looking for some tips on exploring Lake Geneva. You're in for a treat."

Avan leans forward, eager to absorb Marcus's insights. "Absolutely, Marcus. I want to make the most of my time here. What are the top places I should visit?"

Marcus's eyes lit up with enthusiasm. "Well, apart from the natural beauty of the lake and its surrounding parks, you must take leisurely strolls along the historic Lake Shore Path. It offers breathtaking vistas and a glimpse into the area's history. And don't forget to pay a visit to Riviera Beach and its iconic pier. It is a real gem."

Avan nods, soaking in every word. "Thank you, Marcus. I'll be sure to explore those places. I'm eager to immerse myself in the beauty of Lake Geneva."

As the trio continues to chat and make plans, Avan's heart brims with gratitude. Her stay at The Lake House promises not only a magical Christmas party but also the chance to explore the wonders of Lake Geneva, all thanks to Beatrice's warm hospitality and Marcus's invaluable recommendations. This adventure is turning into a cherished chapter in her story.

As the evening sun dips below the horizon, casting a warm, golden glow across the landscape surrounding The Lake House in Lake Geneva, Wisconsin, Avan retreats to her room to change into her festive attire for the highly-anticipated Christmas party. Her heart races with excitement, and she cannot wait to join the revelry downstairs.

She meticulously selects a dress that is both elegant and adorned with just the right touch of holiday flair. She knows Beatrice has mentioned the Christmas sweater tradition, but she cannot resist wearing something a bit more sophisticated for the occasion.

Once she is impeccably dressed and has taken a moment to appreciate her reflection in the mirror, Avan descends the grand staircase that leads to the heart of The Lake House.

She attends the party. The sight that greets her is nothing short of enchanting. The grand hall is bathed in the soft, flickering light of countless candles, casting dancing shadows on the ornate decorations. The air is filled with the delicious aroma of seasonal treats, a tantalising invitation to indulge.

As Avan mingles with the other guests, she cannot help but be captivated by the warmth and camaraderie in the room. She meets new people with fascinating stories to share, each person adding a unique flavour to the evening's festivities.

The Christmas party is a lively affair, with a medley of games, from charades to holiday trivia, keeping everyone entertained. Avan finds herself engaged in animated conversations, clinking glasses with newfound friends, and laughing heartily as she gets to know the wonderful people who have gathered at the hall to celebrate the season.

The hours melt away in a blur of joy and laughter, and before Avan knows it, the clock strikes midnight. The party shows no signs of slowing down, but Avan decides it is time to retreat to her room for a well-deserved rest. She bids her farewells, promising to continue the merriment the next day.

She goes back to the house. As she climbs the stairs, a sense of contentment washes over Avan. The Christmas party is an evening to remember, filled with new connections and cherished memories. She slips into her room, exchanges her festive attire for the comfort of pyjamas, and sinks into the bounce of her cosy bed.

Under the soft glow of her bedside lamp, Avan reflects on the magical night she has just experienced. She cannot help but smile, knowing that the warmth of The Lake House and the wonderful people she has met will linger in her heart for years to come. With a sigh of contentment, she closes her eyes and drifts into a deep and restful sleep, dreaming of more adventures and laughter to come in the enchanting setting of Lake Geneva.

It is a new day. A day which is full of energy. Another memorable day. In the morning, Avan wakes up to the gentle embrace of dawn seeping through the curtains of her room at The Lake House. After a refreshing night's rest, she is eager to begin a new day of adventure. The idea of exploring the picturesque Lake Geneva, Wisconsin, fills her with anticipation.

With a hearty breakfast and a steaming cup of coffee to fortify her, Avan sets off to explore the charming spots that Marcus recommended the night before. She strolls through the quaint streets, each one beckoning her with its unique charm and character.

The morning air feels crisp and invigorating, carrying the scent of pine and the distant allure of the lake's serene waters. As Avan roams through the avenues and corners of this enchanting place, she cannot help but feel like she is walking through a storybook. The cobblestone streets wind their way through historic buildings, each one with a tale of its own to tell.

She makes a stop at the picturesque Lake Shore Path, where the glittering waters of Lake Geneva stretch out before her like a shimmering tapestry. The stunning views and the calmness of her surroundings make her feel like she is in a dream. Avan takes a moment to pause and soak in the sheer beauty of the scene, engraving it into her memory as a moment she will cherish forever.

Following Marcus's recommendations, she visits the iconic Riviera Beach and its charming pier. The sight of boats gently bobbing on the lake's surface and the distant, snow-capped peaks create a picturesque tableau. Avan strolls along the pier, the brisk breeze stinging her cheeks, while she observes the world around her.

As she continues to explore Lake Geneva's hidden gems, Avan encounters friendly locals who greet her with warm smiles, further strengthening her sense of belonging in this idyllic place.

The hours pass by without notice as Avan absorbs the sights and sounds of this charming town. Her heart swells with contentment, and she realises that these moments, the simple pleasures of exploration and discovery, are what make a journey truly memorable.

As the sun ascends higher in the sky, Avan knows it is time to return to The Lake House. She carries with her a heart full of cherished memories, with each corner of Lake Geneva etched into her mind forever. This day of exploration has transformed into a memorable chapter in her life's story, a testament to the magic that can be discovered in the most unexpected of places. "Yet, another day to come and also another adventure to happen. Who knows what tomorrow brings and where I will head?" Avan murmurs to herself on her way back to her room...

Chapter Six

<u>The Winter Holiday Continues, from Aaron's side of the world</u>

A few hours had passed since Aaron got off the phone with Avan, hearing the twists and turns of her day. Her stories spiral out and curve, they are not a straight line, but, Aaron chuckles, he enjoys them. He misses the sound of her voice, the energy and enthusiasm that he always matches. Talking on the phone is the next best thing to being in person. Aaron could tell when Avan was trying to be brave or needed him more than she was willing to admit. That is what is so special and unique about their friendship– [relationship? Love affair? Soul mate status? Who knows. They always refused to be boxed in by a label.] They did not always need words to communicate. There was an understanding to their friendship that everyone noticed: fellow classmates, friends, even strangers. Avan's boyfriend at the time noticed it too, that Aaron and Avan were always inseparable, even when they had the occasional argument, it never lasted more than a day or two. He suspected something was there, especially since that something was so potent. And not only that, but something was there (their connection) long before Avan started dating her boyfriend at the time and long after, too. It was one of those things you cannot really explain, like why the molecules of oil and vinegar do not mix or how a double rainbow forms.

Aaron goes back to sleep and when he wakes up, he decides he is going to travel to Egypt for the vacation for a day or two. Egypt has been on his mind for months or you can say for years, and he wants to seize the day. Yes, he wants to see the old Alexandria library and pyramids and where Naguib Mahfouz was from. How funny it might seem to most people that he is going to ring in a sparkling, brand-new holiday in such an old, ancient place. But not to Avan. Avan is not like most people. Actually, he wants to pick up the phone and invite Avan to spend a day or so in Egypt with him. There is a mixture of feelings in his chest as he puts on his slippers and robe to make coffee. This is what he wants, but should he invite her? We do not always have to act on our impulses in this life. And if she rejects his invitation, will that change their relationship forever? The thought of seeing Avan again after all these years immediately creates a kaleidoscope of emotions in his heart. Nerves and longing mix like the milk he is currently stirring into his cup of coffee. Usually, Aaron is level-headed in front of an entire classroom of youngsters. For his students, he jokes sometimes but is above everything else, put together. If only his students could see him now, puttering around his small room in the city he lives in while packing his bag, plugging in his laptop, booking a flight to Egypt, on edge from the love he has and has had for his dear friend Avan. There are no flowers to pick since it is winter. He remembers what they did as children, picking a petal one by one saying, "She loves me, she loves me not, she loves me..." until the flower answers for you. Aaron does know, actually, but it still feels like he is standing at the edge of a cliff, teetering in the wild. Love is terrifying. Feelings are terrifying.

Aaron sits on the front porch of the room overlooking the steep and beautiful outstretched city, still beautiful even in the winter. He cannot believe what he is about to ask Avan. The phone rings twice.

"Aaron, did you mean to call?" Avan's voice sounds like honey.

"I did actually, although I know we just spoke. How was the Christmas party?" Aaron asks.

"I was there all night, playing chess and trivia and drinking eggnog and dancing and making new friends. Oh, Aaron, I had so much champagne too, they really know how to treat their guests in this little lakeside town. It was so memorable and lovely. I started slurring my words and said good night to everyone. I went back to my room in the cottage, working up the motivation to get under the covers to sleep. The next day, I explored even more hidden gems, hidden nature paths and an abandoned historic barn. I will have to tell you all about it. How about you? Did you have a question for me?" Avan's animated story seamlessly turns into curiosity.

Aaron takes a deep breath. "I am actually going to spend the vacation in Egypt. Would you like to join me there for a couple of days? Do you remember how well we travel together?"

Avan pauses, she is speechless. "Of course, how could I forget?"

Aaron gives her a few beats. "So what do you think? It is crazy of me to ask, I know, but why do people always think of the worst thing that could go wrong instead of the best?"

"You know, Aaron, I would love to join you...but I can't this time. I am so sorry. I wish I could. I am already going to go to Italy in a few weeks for my cousin Hannah's wedding. I wish I had a different answer for you."

"Do not worry. I understand." Aaron lies to her, his heart feels like it is a piece of ice that is cracking off an iceberg and floating down freezing water. They chat for a few more minutes before getting off the phone. Aaron spends the rest of the evening packing, contemplating his invitation in silence, going over how he could have worded it differently. He makes a cup of tea to steady his nerves.

Aaron arrives in Egypt, finally. He made it there in one piece. He does feel tired after the flight, as if under a pile of bricks. But it is not such a strong feeling that a home-cooked meal and a strong black coffee cannot fix. He actually feels overwhelmed and purely happy to be there. There is a symphony of new sounds, smells, and colours in Cairo. New, different street foods to try (Kosharyn and Mulukhiya), carafes of coffee and black tea that have been brewing all day. It is an intense city with lots of animated people who are vibrant in their exchanges even with strangers. Their dialect of Arabic is not quite what Aaron is used to, but nonetheless, not as difficult as Moroccan Arabic. Aaron at first checks into his hostel which is in front of the Great Pyramid of Giza in Giza district. It is a youth hostel since none of the other ones were available on such short notice. Aaron chuckles to himself, *I wonder if it counts that I am young at heart.* After dropping his luggage off, he climbs a lot of stairs to get to find something to eat and a cup of coffee or tea. Egypt welcomes him with open arms, and the people he meets on the streets in Cairo are eager to tell him about places, cities, museums, libraries, and tombstones he simply *must* visit and experience firsthand. Aaron graciously accepts their recommendations and tries not to think about how amazing it would be if Avan was next to him on this one-of-a-kind adventure. At least this way he can blaze the trail, pave the way so to speak and then he and Avan can return another time in the future. He decides after a day or so in Cairo, to travel to Alexandria to see the oldest library in Egypt. As a lifelong bookworm, of course, the library is one of the first things to do on his list. He plans to see the ancient tombstones and museums next, carefully writing down all the details from his day at the end of the day, so as not to forget them, for documentation purposes, and perhaps research, who knows.

Eager to make the most of his day in Alexandria, Aaron wastes no time in setting out to explore the city's must-see attractions. He begins his journey at the majestic Qaitbay Citadel, an imposing fortress that stands as a sentinel over the Mediterranean Sea. As he walks through its ancient stone corridors, he cannot help but feel as if he has stepped back in time. The citadel's towering walls seem to whisper tales of battles and conquests from centuries past.

Next on Aaron's itinerary is the renowned Bibliotheca Alexandrina, a modern marvel that pays homage to the ancient Library of Alexandria. With its striking architecture and the vast collection of books and artefacts, the library is a true testament to human knowledge and achievement. As he wanders through its hallowed halls, Aaron cannot help but marvel at the intellectual legacy that Alexandria has preserved and continues to foster.

Feeling hungry after hours of exploration, Aaron decides to sample some of Alexandria's culinary delights. He finds himself at a charming seaside café, where he indulges in a mezze platter filled with delicacies like hummus, falafel, and baba ganoush. The flavours burst and dance on his tongue, and he cannot resist ordering a second round of mint tea, served in the most elegant glass cup.

With his hunger sated, Aaron continues his adventure by strolling along the picturesque Corniche, a path that hugs the city's coastline. The Mediterranean waves lap gently against the shore, and the sea breeze carries with it the salty scent of adventure. Aaron cannot help but think that life in Alexandria moves at a different pace, one that allows its residents to savour each moment.

As the day wanes, Aaron decides to pay a visit to the Montaza Palace, a regal retreat nestled in lush gardens. The palace's opulent architecture and manicured lawns are a stark contrast to the ancient wonders he had encountered earlier in the day. He gazes at the palace's elegant façade, imagining the royal gatherings and historic moments that have taken place within its walls.

As the sun dips below the horizon, Aaron finds himself at the Alexandria Lighthouse, or what remains of it. Though the towering structure has long since crumbled into the sea, its legacy as one of the Seven Wonders of the Ancient World still looms large. He cannot help but reflect on the impermanence of human achievements and the enduring allure of history.

Exhausted but deeply satisfied, Aaron makes his way back to his hostel in Giza. He drifts off to sleep with the sounds of Alexandria echoing in his mind, knowing that he has experienced a day filled with the magic and wonder of this ancient city.

As he closes his eyes, he whispers to himself, "They say all roads lead to Rome, but today, in Alexandria, I found that all roads lead to history and beauty. A new day is waiting for me in Giza and all around Cairo."

Early morning. As the sun casts its golden rays over the ancient sands of Egypt, Aaron's anticipation soars. He stands at the gateway to history, poised to explore the captivating realms of Giza and Cairo, two of Egypt's crown jewels. His journey promises iconic monuments and timeless mysteries.

Aaron's first destination is the Great Pyramid of Giza, the eternal sentinel of the desert. As he gazes along its colossal limestone blocks, he marvels at the audacity of human ambition. The pyramid's sheer magnitude leaves him in awe, and he cannot help but feel like a tiny speck in the span of humanity. He snaps a photo of himself in front of the pyramid, the quintessential tourist memento.

In his quest for cultural immersion, Aaron ventures to the Khan el-Khalili bazaar in the heart of Cairo. The labyrinthine streets teem with vibrant colours and a cacophony of sounds. The aroma of exotic spices and the chatter of merchants haggling over prices wash over him. Aaron cannot resist buying an intricately designed rug, a keepsake that will forever remind him of his sojourn in the land of pharaohs.

With his rug rolled up and tucked under his arm, Aaron continues his adventure through the city's historical district. He visits the Egyptian Museum, a collage of antiquities that seem to whisper secrets from the past. His eyes skirt across the treasures of Tutankhamun, and he contemplates the significance of artefacts that have survived the battles over time.

To satisfy his intense cravings, Aaron embarks on a culinary adventure. He savours delectable Egyptian dishes such as koshary, a medley of lentils, rice, and pasta drizzled with spicy tomato sauce, and the sweet delights of baklava. Each bite transports him to paradise.

The call to prayer resonates through the air, leading Aaron to the magnificent Sultan Hassan Mosque. Its intricate Islamic architecture bears testimony to the enduring spiritual legacy of Egypt. As he wanders through the courtyard, Aaron finds solace in the tranquil oasis amidst the city's bustling chaos.

The day culminates with a serene sailboat ride on the waters of the Nile. The gentle swaying of the boat on the river's current provides a soothing contrast to the city's frenetic energy. Aaron watches the sun dip below the horizon, casting a rosy hue on the pyramids, a sight that can only be described as surreal.

Exhausted yet fulfilled, Aaron returns to his hostel, his mind abuzz with the memories of a day steeped in history, culture, and wonder. As he drifts into a dreamless slumber, he knows that he has embarked on a journey that transcends time itself.

In the quietness of the night, he whispers to the ancient sands of Egypt, "Today, I walk in the footsteps of pharaohs and revel in the splendour of this timeless land. Tomorrow, I will explore more of your secrets, for Egypt is a treasure trove that never ceases to amaze."

It is 3 am and Aaron is packing for his new journey. He is travelling to a new different city way in the South of the country. After a long journey by car, he arrives in the city. Under the scorching Egyptian sun, Aaron finds himself in the coastal paradise of Hurghada, a city nestled along the shores of the Red Sea. With the promise of adventure and natural beauty, he embarks on a day-long exploration of this idyllic destination, starting with the enchanting Orange Island Bay.

As he steps onto the pristine sands of the bay, Aaron feels like he has entered a dream. The cerulean waters stretch as far as the eye can see, adorned with vibrant coral reefs beneath the surface. He wastes no time donning snorkelling gear and diving into the aquatic wonderland. Among the corals and exotic fish, he swims in a symphony of colours, the world beneath the waves a breathtaking glimpse of marine life.

Emerging from the sea, Aaron's stomach rumbles with hunger. He ventures to a local seafood restaurant, where he indulges in a feast of grilled prawns, calamari, and freshly caught fish, all seasoned with aromatic spices. Each bite is a burst of flavour, a tantalising dance of tastes in his mouth. Reenergized and ready for more exploration, Aaron sets off for Hurghada's marina. The bustling harbour is a vibrant mosaic of fishermen, tourists, and boat enthusiasts. He cannot resist the allure of a traditional Egyptian fishing boat called a "felucca." As the vessel glides through the Red Sea's gentle waves, he savours the salt-tinged breeze and the mesmerising view of the coastline.

Next on his itinerary is a visit to the Giftun Islands, a natural haven of pristine beaches and crystal-clear waters. Time seems to slow down as he relaxes on the powdery sands, the cares of the world fading into the distance.

As the day sinks to evening, Aaron joins a group of fellow travellers on a desert safari. Riding atop a camel, he ventures into the arid expanses of the Eastern Desert, where the rugged terrain and towering dunes create an otherworldly landscape. The sight of the setting sun casting long shadows over the sand dunes is a moment of pure magic.

Returning to Hurghada, Aaron caps off his day with a sumptuous Egyptian meal at a local restaurant. He savours dishes like kofta, falafel, and fattoush, relishing the authentic flavours that fill his nostrils.

Back at his hotel, he gazes out at the Red Sea one last time, the moonlight casting a silvery glow upon the water. As he drifts into a contented slumber, he cannot help but reflect on the incredible experiences of the day.

In the tranquil stillness of the night, Aaron whispers to the stars, "Hurghada, you've shown me a world of wonder and beauty. Tomorrow, I'll continue my journey, knowing that Egypt has truly stolen a piece of my heart."

It is an early morning even before sunlight, "Hurray, another day with another city, I am all packed and I have my breakfast box with me; the bus is ready. Pop on the bus and pop out in another ancient city" Aaron murmured and chuckled. After 7 hours of driving, he arrives in the next city. As the sun bathes the ancient city of Luxor in a warm, golden glow, Aaron's footsteps echo through its historic streets. Luxor, often referred to as the "world's greatest open-air museum," holds an unparalleled allure, and he is determined to fully immerse himself in it.

His day begins at the awe-inspiring Karnak Temple, a sprawling complex of grandeur that seems to defy the passage of centuries. As he wanders through the colossal columns and intricately carved hieroglyphs, Aaron cannot help but marvel at the ancient Egyptians' architectural prowess. He whispers to himself, "They truly built monuments that withstand the test of time."

Next, Aaron finds himself before the iconic Luxor Temple, its illuminated statues guarding the entrance. The temple's majesty is a testament to Egypt's enduring legacy. As he explores its hallowed halls, he cannot shake the feeling of being transported through millennia.

His journey continues to the Valley of the Kings, where the silent guardians of pharaohs' tombs lie beneath the desert sands. The grandeur of the tombs leaves him humbled, and he ponders the mysteries that continue to shroud the lives of these ancient rulers.

But amid the grandeur and history, a pang of loneliness strikes Aaron. He finds a quiet corner in the shade and speaks to himself in a soft voice, "Avan, my love, I wish you were here with me. These wonders are so much more meaningful when shared with you. I miss you desperately, and every monument I see reminds me of you."

His yearning for Avan lingers as he visits the majestic Hatshepsut's Temple, perched elegantly against the cliffs. The temple's architectural grace mirrors the strength and determination of the female pharaoh it pays its respects to. Aaron cannot help but admire the magnitude of Hatshepsut's reign.

As the day wears on, Aaron journeys to the bustling Luxor market, a vibrant array of colours, scents, and sounds. The merchants' calls and the aroma of exotic spices wash over him, momentarily diverting his thoughts from his beloved. He purchases a small trinket, a token of his travels to remind him of Avan.

His final stop is the tranquil Luxor Corniche, where the Nile River flows serenely. The sun begins its descent, casting a warm, golden hue over the waters. Aaron watches the boats sail by and feels a sense of tranquillity in the presence of the ancient river.

Returning to his hotel, Aaron's mind returnings to Avan. He speaks to the stars in the night sky hoping she will hear, "My dearest Avan, I carry you with me in every step of this journey. I long for the day when we can explore these wonders together, for you are the missing piece of my adventure."

As he closes his eyes and drifts into slumber, the ancient city of Luxor whispers its secrets, and Aaron finds solace in the dreams that connect him with the love he so dearly misses.

As the boat heads downstream on the Nile River, Aaron's gaze is fixed on the horizon. The journey from Luxor to Aswan promises new adventures and discoveries, but his heart carries a constant companion – thoughts of Avan. With each passing mile, the river whispers its stories, and Aaron's musings turn increasingly romantic.

The boat docks in Aswan, a city resplendent with natural beauty and cultural treasures. As he steps on to the bustling riverfront, Aaron feels a sense of anticipation. He has heard tales of Aswan's enchantments, and today, he is determined to experience them all.

His first stop is the Philae Temple, an ancient marvel dedicated to the goddess Isis. As he explores the temple's intricate reliefs and statues, he cannot help but relate the enduring love between Isis and Osiris to his own longing for Avan. In a hushed voice, he murmurs to himself, "Just as their love transcended time, so does mine for you, Avan." Who knows whether this is out of love or another degree of missing someone?

Next on his itinerary is the colossal Aswan High Dam, a modern engineering marvel that tames the mighty Nile. The dam's imposing presence contrasts with the serene river, serving as a symbol of human ingenuity and determination. Aaron reflects on the power of love and determination, certain that one day, he and Avan will overcome the distance that separates them. They must. They have nothing to lose.

A boat's white sails billow in the breeze, and Aaron watches the water ripple under the golden sun. He cannot help but imagine himself and Avan on a similar voyage, their love as boundless as the river.

A visit to the Nubian Village allows Aaron to immerse himself in the local culture. He samples traditional Nubian cuisine and shares stories with the welcoming villagers. Their warmth and hospitality remind him of the depth of connection he yearns for with Avan.

As the day wanes and the sun dips below the horizon, Aaron finds himself at the serene Elephantine Island. The tranquil beauty of the island's botanical gardens offers a moment of peace. He sits by the water's edge, watching the river flow, and whispers to the stars, "Avan, each moment without you feels like an eternity. But like the Nile that continues its course, our love flows ceaselessly."

At twilight, Aaron visits the enchanting Unfinished Obelisk, a testament to the grand ambitions of ancient Egypt. He cannot help but draw a parallel to the grand dreams he shares with Avan, knowing that they, too, are a work in progress.

Returning to the boat, Aaron's thoughts have transformed into a romantic reverie. As he sails around the city, he is filled with hope and determination. In his heart, he knows that the distance between him and Avan is temporary, and their love is as enduring as the ancient sands of Egypt.

Aaron finds himself once again navigating the realm of airports and aeroplanes, bidding farewell to the timeless land of Egypt and setting his sights on the Kurdish region of Sulaymaniyah. The flight from Aswan International Airport to Cairo International Airport marks the beginning of his journey to a different corner of the world.

As the plane soars above the vast Egyptian landscape, Aaron's mind is a kaleidoscope of memories from his Egyptian adventure. He cannot help but reflect on the awe-inspiring monuments he has explored, the ancient temples and bustling markets that have left an indelible mark on his soul.

Seated by the window, he gazes out at the golden sands and winding Nile River, a final farewell to Egypt's ancient beauty. The view from the plane is a testament to the country's rich history and enduring allure.

During the flight, Aaron indulges in a cup of aromatic coffee and delves into the pages of a captivating book. The words transport him to distant worlds and provide a welcome distraction from the miles that separate him from Avan.

As the plane cruises above the azure waters of the Mediterranean, Aaron's thoughts turn to his beloved. He whispers to the empty seat beside him, "Oh, Avan, how I wish you were here with me. Egypt's wonders, the Nile's tranquillity, and the bustling streets – all would be more vibrant with your presence."

Between chapters of his book, Aaron peruses the in-flight entertainment options. He promises himself to write a Novel about this enjoyable journey. Then, he decides to watch a few movies, letting the cinematic tales whisk him away to different realities. The films offer a brief respite from his thoughts of Avan, but they cannot extinguish the yearning he feels.

The flight from Cairo International Airport to Sulaymaniyah International Airport passes in a blur of clouds and distant horizons. Aaron's anticipation for his next destination mingles with a lingering sense of nostalgia for Egypt.

As the plane touches down in Sulaymaniyah, he disembarks with a heart heavy with longing. The journey has taken him from the wonders of Egypt to a new chapter in his adventure, but the desire to share it all with Avan remains as strong as ever. He puts his first step on Kurdish land (his homeland) and he tells himself quoting from Neil Armstrong "One small step for man, one giant leap for mankind."...

Chapter Seven

<u>Aaron goes to Florence</u>

As the plane touches down in Sulaymaniyah, he disembarks with a
heart heavy with longing. The journey has taken him from the wonders of
Egypt to a new chapter in his adventure, but the desire to share it all with
Avan remains as strong as ever. He takes his first step on Kurdish land, his homeland.

When he returns to his flat, he jangles his keys from his bag and unlocks the door, a somewhat tricky mission. It's an old wooden door and one must press their body weight on it fully for it to open. You might as well say open sesame. Aaron walks through his front door and locks it. Nothing in his flat has changed apart from a light blue textured glass vase of flowers that are now wilted, their dead petals gathered around the object in the form of a circle. His furniture, coat rack, and framed artwork are all satisfyingly familiar and now changed, somehow. Time in Egypt gave Aaron a sense of wonder, like a child who is mesmerised about bubbles. Aaron unrolls the rug he bought at the Egyptian souq and decides to decorate it under his coffee table in his living room. Rugs really do tie the room together. Then, he sets his luggage in his bedroom. He suddenly feels a clear sense of what he wants to do, clear as a mirror's reflection or how a loved one sees you, sometimes more clearly than you can see yourself. He wants to travel to Florence, Italy. He wants to see Avan, and the desire to share everything with her remains as strong as the coffee he makes. It is a want that consumes him like no other craving. It has lasted years. That is the thing, time does not heal all wounds. And to use the word heal implies that the trauma has ended. A separation from Avan feels like suffering, and feeling like he cannot stand it any longer, Aaron plans to go to Florence. *I will surprise her,* Aaron brims with effervescence at his own thought, suddenly emboldened with a twist of whimsy.

On the plane to Florence, Aaron sits biting his nails and playing with his hair. *I hope I can find her.* He thinks. *Is this crazy? Is this a mistake? Do I know any words in Italian?* But deep down, he knows it is now or never, and the latter he will regret for the rest of his life. Regardless or not if Avan mistakenly called him, the call set off a domino effect of feelings, memories, and their imaginations that both Avan and Aaron carefully placed on a shelf in the safest of places terribly close to their hearts which cannot be ignored. There is just no getting over the type of love and connection they shared and continue to share. This is what propelled Aaron to make the spontaneous decision to travel to Florence. And even if he does not catch her, at least he will get a chance to traverse around Italy and see it with his own eyes.

The air in the airplane is stale by the time the plane lands, and Aaron feels a bit groggy and out of it. Once he steps off the plane, he finds a payphone and with shaky hands dials her number. Finally, after years, they are in the same time zone, in the same country. He has no luck. He is here! In Florence! It is gorgeous and Aaron keeps blinking just to make sure he is not dreaming. It is real life indeed, and he thinks, *and hopefully, I can find my friend.* His mixed emotions are all over the place, like confetti that gets everywhere or sand from a beach towel.

Aaron spruces himself up, even spritzing himself with a bit of cologne. He wears a winter jacket with a scarf and brand-new Sperry shoes for walking. He tried calling Avan before showering, and now glancing at his phone again, she still has not returned his call. How funny it is that they are still playing "phone tag" in the same country, Aaron chortles to himself. He is going to join a Sunset Walking Tour in Florence which includes wine and food tasting. As he is about to leave, Avan calls him back.

"Guess where I am?" Aaron says when she answers the phone.

"The moon?" Avan teases him.

"Guess again," Aaron says coyly.

"Siberia?" Avan jokes.

"You must be cold if you keep suggesting cold places, dearest Avan. I am in Italy. Surprise. Did you still need a date for your cousin's wedding?"

On the other end of the line, Avan shrieks in joy, yells playfully, and then stops in her tracks.

"Are you really here, Aaron?"

"I came to see you. Thought you could use some company exploring, and for the wedding."

"Yes, yes, a hundred times yes. A thousand times yes. A thousand and one times yes, like that book you were reading the first time we went to that dusty bookshop, *A Thousand and One Nights*."

"The one you asked to see and then could not put down? You were so immersed in it; I tried to get your attention so many times." Aaron fondly recalls that rainy day.

The rest of their conversation buzzed and flowed like honey. They could feel their molecules and breath more viscerally, and felt a heightened sense of safety. Aaron tells Avan about the Sunset Walking Tour he is on his way to, and she says she will meet him there, and afterwards, maybe they could sit at a bar and plan out their Italy adventure in more detail over a glass of wine or beer, if Aaron agreed and liked the idea. Or a mug of hot brewed coffee.

On the Sunset Walking Tour, Avan's dark brown curly hair looked golden in the sultry rays of the setting sun. Aaron could barely pay any attention to the tour guide or anyone else around him, only hearing bits and pieces of his spiels on the architectural histories in Florence. Florence was absolutely stunningly beautiful, and Avan seemed really happy there. Every cobblestone, building, cart, window, was bathed in a golden hue at this magical hour of the day.

There was an exuberance to Avan's step. Aaron could not stop sneaking looks to her, and eagerly awaited the end of the tour so that they could be alone in their own company. She tasted a Chianti wine that was life changing. The flavour of the wine deeply improved over time, the tour guide mentioned, gently pleasing the small crowd of tourists who were all holding paper maps, sunglasses, and disposable cameras. Of course, Avan had her Canon DSLR camera around her neck, lovingly restored for this trip. She said she was happy her cousin did not ask her to be the official wedding photographer so she could simply attend the wedding, enjoy, and have fun. Aaron kept trying to read Avan's facial expressions. Did his arrival in Italy startle her? What should they do? Where are they going to go from here, both geographically in the beautiful country of Italy, but also where are they going to go in their relationship, romantic friendship, what was to become? The future was here, knocking, holding a glass of wine for them, and needing an answer quite soon.

Aaron and Avan walk through the enchanted streets of Florence, letting the breathtaking architecture that surrounds them sink in. The historic buildings stand tall, whispering secrets from the past and the cobblestone streets exude an old-world charm unique to this particular city.

They share their admiration for the city's rich history, which seems like a tapestry woven with threads of art, culture, and politics. Florence's past is alive in its presence, and it feels like they took a step back in time.

Avan asks if Aaron has seen the David statue at the Accademia Gallery, and Aaron mentions it is on his to-do list. The David is renowned as a masterpiece, symbolizing human potential and beauty. Avan raves about the incredible detail and craftsmanship of Michelangelo, encouraging Aaron to visit the Uffizi Gallery as well, where the collection of Renaissance art is beyond compare.

Excited about their cultural explorations, the friends shift their attention to the culinary delights of Florence to accompany their explorations. Aaron confesses his love for Italian cuisine, particularly rotini pasta and limoncello gelato. Avan wholeheartedly agrees, calling it a culinary dream come true, and recommends trying the famous ribollita soup to truly taste Florence. It is love at first bite.

Amidst their conversations, they discuss the weather, with Aaron inquiring about the city's winter. Avan explains that she has been fortuitous so far with mild weather during her stay, making her walks enjoyably pleasant.

As they stroll through the streets, they feel the gentle breeze on their faces and playfully on the napes of their necks and they savour the floral scent of fresh flowers in the air. Aaron mentions that it feels like the universe itself conspired to make this trip unforgettable.

Avan appreciates Aaron's eloquence and adds that it is not just the scenery but also the company that makes this trip special. Shared moments, laughter, and the joy of discovering new places together create an experience that money cannot buy.

In a toast to their friendship and adventures, they raise their glasses, one with wine and one with coffee, clinking them together, and Avan says, "Here is to many more adventures, laughter, and gelato in Florence."

Aaron echoes, "Cheers, Avan! Florence, we're here to savour every moment, one beautiful street at a time."

As Aaron and Avan continue their leisurely walk through the picturesque streets of Florence, they find a charming little cafe with outdoor seating and decide to take a break. Sipping their espresso and taking in the atmosphere, the conversation shifts to their lives back in their respective home countries. Soft 'Nature-Forest Relaxing Music' is playing in the background of their talk.

Aaron says, "Life here in Italy is different compared to my hometown in Kurdistan. The pace is slower, and people seem to take more time to savour the moment."

Avan chuckles and says, "You're right, Aaron. Life in the US is bustling, and the pace can be quite frantic at times. But it has its own charm, and there is always something happening. It is a land of contrasts, much like the streets of Florence."

Aaron continues, "Speaking of contrasts, I remember that time back in China when we went on that crazy road trip along the coast. The rugged cliffs, the endless ocean, and the freedom of the open road. That was unforgettable."

Avan chuckles again and says, "Oh, that road trip was a blast! And remember the night we stayed in that cosy little beachside cabin, we were watching the stars and talking about our dreams and aspirations? Those are the moments I will never forget."

Aaron says, "I'll never forget that night, Avan. It is moments like those that make life truly memorable. And it is incredible how our paths crossed in a foreign land, and we became such great friends. It is a miracle."

Avan nods and adds, "Fate has a funny way of bringing people together, doesn't it? It is like we are meant to share these experiences. It's funny how a cup of coffee in Florence makes us reminisce about our adventures back then."

Aaron smiles and says, "You're absolutely right. Life is a collection of moments, and I'm grateful for each one we share. Whether it's hiking through the Blue Mountains or drinking espresso in Tuscany, the memories we create together are priceless." He starts laughing out loud and bends over, holding his hand on his belly, to the degree that people at the neighbouring tables look puzzled.

Avan raises his cup and says, "Coffee-Cheers to that, Aaron. May we continue to create more memories and share more adventures, in Florence and beyond."

As they clink their coffee cups together in a toast, the friends cherish their shared history and look forward to many more chapters in their journey together, wherever it might take them.

Avan and Aaron have been friends for years, sharing stories, laughter, and sometimes even a few heated arguments. They sit in a cosy cafe, sipping on their steaming cups of coffee, and the air is filled with the rich aroma of roasted beans. The conversation flows smoothly, touching on everything from work to hobbies to memories. Avan has something important to discuss, and she can't hold it back any longer.

"Hey, Aaron," Avan begins with a smile, her eyes sparkling with anticipation. "Do you remember my cousin?"

Aaron takes a sip of his coffee, his brow furrowed in thought. "Who? The one who lives in Chicago or the one in New York?"

Avan nods enthusiastically. "That's the one! She used to. For now, she is getting married tomorrow, and her wedding party is going to be amazing. It's a big deal for our family, she is the first cousin to get married, and I'd love for you to be there with me."

Aaron looks hesitant, shifting in his seat. "I appreciate the invitation, Avan, but I've got a lot on my plate these few days. I came to see you and Italy also. Many places to visit and many cities to see and all that."

Avan's enthusiasm turns to disappointment, her eyes narrowing slightly. "Come on, Aaron. You know how important this is to me. It's family, and I really want you to be there."

Aaron can sense the tension in the air and sighs. "Look, Avan, I get it. But I can't promise anything right now. Let me think about it, okay?"

Avan can't hide her frustration, and her voice carries a tinge of annoyance. "Think about it? Aaron, this is important to me, and I thought you'd want to share these moments with me."

Aaron feels a pang of guilt as he watches Avan's face fall. He reaches out to touch her hand. "I don't mean to upset you, Avan. Let's not argue about this, okay? I'll do my best to make it work, alright?"

Avan's expression softens as she meets Aaron's gaze. "Promise?"

Aaron nods, his eyes filled with sincerity. "Promise. I'll be there with you at your cousin's wedding party."

Avan's face lights up with joy, and she leans over to give Aaron a warm hug. "You're the best, Aaron! This means a lot to me."

Aaron chuckles and returns the hug, relieved that he could put a smile back on Avan's face. "I'd do anything for you, Avan. I'm looking forward to celebrating with your family." He smiles and says "Well anything, but not everything, you are tricky enough to know what I mean," he starts to laugh.

The evening stars, like the paintings of Vincent Van Gogh, and bathes the cafe in a warm, bright glow, Avan and Aaron continue their conversation, the earlier tension forgotten, and their friendship stronger than ever.

They leave the Café while they are having their Americanos in disposable cups. Aaron and Avan stroll through the charming streets of Florence, the crisp February air nipping at their cheeks. The city's historic beauty surrounds them as they wander through alleys lined with ancient buildings, marvelling at the timeless architecture and the breathtaking artistry of this Italian gem. They feel like children again, in awe of everything.

Avan, always eager to explore, cannot contain her excitement. "Aaron, isn't Florence just enchanting? I feel so lucky to be here with you."

Aaron smiles warmly, his eyes reflecting the splendour of their surroundings. "Absolutely, Avan. This city is like a work of art in itself, and it's even better with your company."

As they continue their walk, Aaron feels a stirring within him, something he has been hesitant to share. He's always treasured their friendship, but over time, something more has blossomed, something he keeps hidden, deep within.

Avan senses a change in Aaron's demeanour and decides to take a step forward. "You know, Aaron, it's not just the city that's beautiful. Our friendship means the world to me."

Aaron looks at Avan, his eyes revealing a mixture of emotions. "Avan, I feel the same way. You're an incredible friend, and I cherish our moments together."

Avan's voice grows softer, more intimate. "Aaron, there's something I want to say. I've been thinking about our friendship a lot lately."

Aaron feels his heart race, but he remains composed, urging her to continue. "What's on your mind, Avan?"

She takes a deep breath and looks deep into his eyes. "I value our friendship immensely, but I can't help feeling there's something more here. I've felt it for a while, and I just need to know, do you feel it too?"

Aaron is taken aback, surprised by Avan's candidness, yet relieved that the unspoken has finally been voiced. "Avan, I can't deny that there's something special between us, something beyond friendship. I've felt it too."

They walk on, their hearts now unburdened, the weight of their unspoken emotions lifted. Florence's romantic aura seems to intensify, weaving a golden backdrop to their newfound honesty.

As they meander through Florence's picturesque streets, they know that their friendship has evolved, and it is time to explore what lies beyond. The city, with its timeless beauty, has become the perfect setting for the beginning of a new chapter in their lives.

The enchanting streets of Florence are illuminated under the moon as Avan and Aaron continue tracing the steps of their night-time stroll. The city's charm appears to grow stronger with each hour, swirling romance around them.

Avan, with a mischievous sparkle in her eye, turns to Aaron. "Aaron, how about making this night one for the books? Why don't you join me for the remainder of the night?"

Aaron, captivated by her proposal, meets her gaze. "You know, Avan, that's a splendid idea. I'd cherish it."

And so, the night progresses, carrying them along. They saunter through Florence's cobblestone streets, swapping stories, diving into romantic conversations, and now and then, dropping by a café for more steaming coffee. Time appears to dissipate as they laugh, reminisce, and savour the city's beauty.

As the clock edges closer to 3 a.m., Aaron knows it is time to draw the curtains on their enchanting night. He takes Avan's hand gently and says, "Avan, you've got a big day ahead with your cousin's wedding party. You need your rest and preparation. I must return to my hotel as well."

Avan's expression hints at reluctance; she wants to keep the night going. "Can't we extend our time, Aaron? I don't want this night to end. I hate saying goodbye. Especially to you."

Aaron, his voice tender and understanding, responds, "I'd love to, Avan, but we both need our rest. Tomorrow's significant, and we need to be in top form. I promise we'll meet again soon."

Reluctantly, Avan agrees, and they head to her place. The lobby of her hotel serves as the backdrop for their farewell, a moment that is bittersweet. Aaron gives her a lingering hug, reaches and strokes her cheek, and as they part, their eyes meet with a silent pact. He watches her vanish into the building, a smile gracing his face, and then makes his way back to his hotel.

The memory of that night in Florence, the shared moments, and their newfound connection linger with them as they prepare for the significant day that awaits.

Aaron finds himself back in his hotel room, feeling refreshed after taking a shower and preparing his clothes for the upcoming marriage party tomorrow. The city of Florence lies still outside, its twinkling lights painting a captivating picture through his window. He settles into his bed, switches off the lights, and gazes out of the window at the starry canvas above.

As he stares at the heavens, Aaron's thoughts drift to Avan and the moments they have shared. He ponders what to say to her tomorrow, considering where to invite her after the party and which other charming Italian cities they should explore together. Memories race through his mind like shooting stars, and he cannot help but feel that their time together is too precious to be fleeting.

Lying in the dim glow of Florence's night sky, Aaron contemplates the adventures that lie ahead, the chapters of their life waiting to be written, and the everlasting memories they will collect. Gradually, he drifts into slumber, his dreams filled with visions of their shared journeys and anticipation of what the future holds for them.

Chapter Eight

<u>Hannah's Wedding and the escape to their next adventure</u>

The day of Hannah's wedding has finally arrived. The party was not until the afternoon, after a private ceremony at the *Villa di Maiano* in the grand ballroom with the antique chandelier. Avan reached out her arms like wings to stretch, letting out a big yawn and cracking her back. The bed she slept in was not one she was accustomed to.

Finally, the future has arrived. Avan, albeit a bundle of nerves, could not deny the excitement fizzing in her chest. She got dressed slowly, choosing to wear Monstera leaf earrings, all solid gold of course for the occasion, to match a princess dress, a long flowing silky pink dress threaded with gold. Her nails matched and she added some silver rings and iridescent bangles to the ensemble. She would wear patent leather wedge heels but bring high-top converses just in case her and Aaron get bored of schmoozing at the party and need to skulk off and jump over a fence or something. They absolutely discussed, over wine and coffee, travelling to Rome, the Vatican, Tuscany, and Venice, and bits and pieces of their conversation came back to Avan in waves.

Her thoughts were of Aaron. She could think about him for hours, like when she used to visit Garfield Park Conservatory in Chicago and sit by the koi fish pond, watching the speckled orange, black, and yellow koi fish give the whole pond a show, slinking around each other, each one like tiny beautiful globes of abstract art. Aaron is like a musical composition that few took the time to learn by heart.

There are so many family members that are going to be there that Avan had not seen in years. Avan felt a slight pang of guilt at having a conflicted emotion. Today is Friday, a sacred day for both Muslim and Jewish people. It is Shabbat for Jews. It is Friday Pray for the Muslims. As happy as she feels for Hannah, she could not help but wonder when, and if, she is ever going to get married. The Villa di Maiano was something out of a fantasy picture book. When Avan arrived with curled, mascaraed eyelashes and make-up, she found Aaron, standing sturdy, waiting for her at the gated entrance of this vista. Behind Aaron, waiters in tuxedos circulated with glasses of Prosecco, Italian sparkling wine, Italian iced coffee, and food.

"Perhaps would you care to meet me under this cypress tree before we go in and block me so my family members do not see me smoking a cigarette?" Avan asked Aaron with a mischievous look in her eyes.

"Of course, signora" Aaron says, playing along. Aaron cleans up well, truly. What a dish. He is even adorning Tanzanite cufflinks and leather shoes for this occasion, for a wedding of whom he has never even met the bride and groom! Avan takes a long drag from her cigarette and looks out to the hilltop vista. The sun is cosily situated in the bluish sky casting a golden, scintillating hue onto the hilly rows of cypress trees, and the dim glow of Florence's night sky will soon be above the waltzing crowd, their cheeks rosy from the champagne.

Oddly enough, Avan and Aaron feel shy around each other. It is as if suddenly they are all dressed up, and almost like strangers side by side, uncomfortable in the high heels and starched button-downs and tassel loafer shoes. Avan looks as glamorous as a movie star, smoking a cigarette in lipstick. She is taking her time with it to enjoy it herself, and Aaron provides a sort of soothing comfort and presence, in addition to blocking her from her family's view. A lot of her family are doctors and she does not want them to find out she smokes cigarettes. Although, for the record, she barely smokes. Once in a blue moon. Aaron is studying his shoes, lost in thought, furrowing his brows as she does.

The pair sneak into the side of the stone venue before anyone notices Avan is not there.

"AVAN! YOU CAME!" Hannah, Avan's cousin, shrieks and runs toward her to hug her. She is stunning. She has a tiara and daisy flowers braided into her hair. Her wedding dress is long-sleeved, the top is lace and the bottom is chiffon, and it swirls as she walks.

"Have you met Duccio, my husband?" Hannah asks Avan.

"I do not believe so. I am Avan. A pleasure to meet you. And this is my...friend Aaron." Avan reaches to her right side but Aaron is not there. It looks like Hannah and Avan's grandmother have swooped in to converse with Aaron and ask him all sorts of questions. Hannah and Avan look at each other with a knowing look, knowing that Grandma is about to pin him to a corner and talk his ear off. Although she is 86, she still loves to talk about documentaries, French films, public policy, local politics, anything and everything.

Avan has a ploy. She excuses herself and slinks over to Aaron and her grandma.

"Aaron, do you know where we are seated? Can we go over there and put our things down?" Aaron smiles. The three go down to sit at the table and wait for the seafood dinner to be served.

"Where should we go next?" Aaron leans over and whispers to Avan.

"I am thinking somewhere on the coast, and then Sicily?" Avan whispers excitedly, holding onto his forearm for dear life.

They enjoy the wedding party, meeting uncles, aunts, cousins, and friends, tasting assorted desserts and foods, scotch and old-fashioned and enjoying the jazz band playing outside. After several hours, they pull an Irish goodbye and head off privately to continue their trip, starting in Rome.

The moon hangs luminously over the ancient cobblestone streets of Florence, casting a soft glow upon the silhouettes of Aaron and Avan as they stroll away from the enchanting ambience of Hannah's wedding. The echoes of celebration resonate in the air, and the crisp Italian night holds promises of an unforgettable adventure for the two companions.

Aaron, with his tailored suit exuding timeless elegance, and Avan, donning a sophisticated gown that mirrors the grace of the surrounding Renaissance architecture, meander through narrow alleys adorned with walls climbing with ivy and charming rustic facades. The city, with its palpable history and artistic allure, seems to embrace them in a captivating dance of culture and romance.

As they amble along the Arno River, its waters shimmering in the moonlight, their footsteps meld seamlessly with the distant strains of a serenading violin. Florence, a nocturnal masterpiece, unfolds its charms, revealing secrets and stories etched in every stone and archway.

The duo finds themselves captivated by the allure of a quaint gelato shop tucked away in a hidden corner. With an air of indulgence, they savour artisanal flavours that speak of centuries-old recipes, each spoonful transporting them deeper into the heart of Italian culinary craftsmanship. The symphony of taste and texture complements the rich tapestry of the city's nighttime ambience.

The Ponte Vecchio, adorned with golden lights, beckons them to traverse its ancient arches. High above the river, they marvel at the juxtaposition of tradition and modernity, the city lights playing upon the waters like a celestial ballet.

Their conversation is a melange of intellectual discourse and whimsical banter which resonates with the intellectual curiosity that binds them. From the echoes of Renaissance poets to contemporary musings on art and life, Aaron and Avan weave a verbal tapestry that mirrors the rich cultural heritage surrounding them.

As the night presses on, Florence embraces them in its timeless embrace. From the bustling Piazza della Signoria to the hushed corners of the Uffizi Gallery, every step reveals a new facet of the city's mystique. The fragrance of blooming jasmine flowers meshes with the subtle aroma of aged leather from antiquarian bookshops, creating an olfactory symphony that accompanies their nocturnal odyssey.

As the first rays of dawn paint the sky in hues of rose and gold, Aaron and Avan find themselves atop the Piazzale Michelangelo, overlooking the city that has been their moonlit playground. The dawn seems to whisper promises of new beginnings and everlasting memories, etched into their collective shared experience.

In the quiet of the early morning, with the city still draped in the remnants of night, Aaron and Avan share a moment of quiet reflection. A timeless friendship, some could say a friend-love relationship, finds new depth in the embrace of Florence, and as they descend from the heights of Piazzale Michelangelo, the echoes of their laughter and the warmth of their camaraderie linger in the air, a testament to a night that transcends the ordinary and becomes a chapter in the story of their enduring connection.

Dawn casts its ethereal glow upon Florence, and Aaron and Avan, their hearts still echoing the city's nocturnal serenade, decide to embark on a journey beyond its borders. The train station, a bustling nexus of departures and arrivals, welcomes them into its grandeur, the rhythmic clatter of wheels against tracks promising new adventures in the heart of Italy.

As they navigate the intricate web of train schedules and platforms, their anticipation grows palpable. The destination board, adorned with the names of Italy's most romantic and storied cities, beckons like a treasure map promising glimpses of cultural splendour.

Their first stop is Venice, the city of winding canals and timeless romance. As the train glides effortlessly across the Venetian lagoon, Aaron and Avan find themselves entranced by the ethereal beauty of the city rising from the water. Strolling through narrow alleys and crossing ornate bridges, they lose themselves in the labyrinthine charm of Venice, where every corner seems to harbour secrets of love and history.

Next on their itinerary is Verona, a city steeped in Shakespearean lore. The train's gentle rhythm carries them to the famed balcony of Juliet, where they revel in the timeless tale of star-crossed lovers. Verona's ancient amphitheatre, with its well-preserved grandeur, echoes with the whispers of bygone performances and love stories etched in stone.

Their journey continues to the majestic city of Florence's counterpart, Rome. The Eternal City unfolds before them like an open-air museum, each cobblestone street and monumental ruin testifying to centuries of civilization. From the grandeur of the Colosseum to the sacred quietude of the Vatican City, Aaron and Avan immerse themselves in the richness of Rome's historical tapestry.

Naples, with its vibrant street life and the looming presence of Mount Vesuvius, awaits them as the final chapter of their Italian odyssey. The train winds its way through picturesque landscapes, revealing the allure of the Amalfi Coast and the tantalizing aroma of Neapolitan cuisine. Aaron and Avan, savouring the essence of each city they visit, discover the unique romance woven into the fabric of Italian culture.

As they retrace their steps to Florence, the journey back holds a bittersweet note. The train, now a vessel of memories and shared experiences, carries them through the scenic vistas of Tuscany. The Tuscan hills, bathed in the golden hues of the setting sun, mirror the warmth of their travel-weary yet fulfilled hearts.

Arriving back in Florence, the duo realises that their Italian sojourn has not just been a series of destinations but a narrative of shared moments and cultural immersion. The echoes of their laughter, the snapshots of ancient cities, and the indelible connection forged through the journey linger as an ode to the timeless romance of Italy—a journey that transcends time, much like the love stories engraved in the annals of the cities they explore.

Sitting in a fine-dine Italian restaurant, its ambience steeped in the aroma of simmering sauces and the soft glow of ambient lighting, Aaron and Avan bask in the warmth of their post-journey reverie. The strains of an acoustic guitar serenade them, weaving a melodic backdrop to the tales of their Italian escapade.

As they read the menu, a veritable symphony of culinary delights, memories of their travels dance in their eyes. The waitstaff, attired in classic Italian elegance, introduces them to a gastronomic journey that mirrors their recent expedition through the heart of Italy. The clinking of fine glassware and the chatter of fellow patrons create a backdrop that amplifies the romantic ambience.

The dishes, a culinary ode to the diverse regions they explore, arrive at their table with an artful presentation that befits the canvas of Florence itself. Each bite transports them back to the bustling markets of Naples, the savoury flavours of Veronese cuisine, and the delicate nuances of Venetian seafood. Their conversation becomes a mosaic, seamlessly blending tales of ancient ruins with the savouring of freshly made pasta.

Amidst the feast, Aaron and Avan find solace in reflections on their journey. The familiar cities they think they know unfold in a new light, revealing hidden treasures and deepening their appreciation for Italy's rich cultural tapestry.

Avan, her eyes aglow with the reflections of flickering candlelight, recounts the beauty of the Colosseum under a moonlit sky, while Aaron shares the awe-inspiring moments spent gazing at Michelangelo's David in Florence.

The conversation, a delicate dance between romantic musings and the camaraderie forged through shared exploration, enriches their bond. The nuances of their laughter, the exchange of knowing glances, and the shared nostalgia for moments only they witness intertwine seamlessly with the symphony of flavours.

As they delve into a decadent tiramisu, the conversation takes a reflective turn. Avan, her voice a harmonious melody, expresses how this journey is more than a mere exploration of cities—it is a celebration of their friendship, a strengthening of the ties that bind them. Aaron, his gaze fixed upon the city lights visible through the restaurant's window, echoes the sentiment, acknowledging the profound impact of shared adventures on their connection.

The night unfolds like a tapestry, each course a chapter in the story of their Italian odyssey. With dessert plates cleared and the last notes of the guitar fading into the restaurant's ambience, Aaron and Avan linger in the moment. The restaurant, a sanctuary of culinary artistry, becomes the stage for the finale of their Italian escapade—a journey not just through cities and landscapes but through the labyrinth of their hearts and the corridors of their enduring friendship.

Coffee at last. Amidst the lingering aroma of espresso/americano and the flickering candlelight, Avan's eyes sparkle with inspiration as she gazes at Aaron across the table. The soft strains of Italian music provide a backdrop to their conversation, a discussion that evolves into a new chapter of their journey.

Avan, leaning forward, says "Aaron, can you imagine encapsulating the essence of our Italian odyssey in a book? A narrative that breathes life into the cities we explore and the bond we cultivate?"

Aaron, smiling, answers back "Avan, that's a splendid idea. I always believe in the power of storytelling, and our journey is a tale worth sharing. What do you envision for our book?"

Avan, thoughtfully, adds "Picture this—a narrative that weaves together the tapestry of our experiences, capturing not just the picturesque landscapes but the emotions, the laughter, and the nuances that make each city uniquely enchanting."

Aaron, nodding, adds "I love the idea of immersing our readers in the cultural mosaic of Italy. It's not just about the landmarks but the moments that transform our perspective. How do we structure the book?"

Avan, leaning back, gesturing, starts to speak "I imagine a chronological approach, beginning with the enchantment of Florence and then navigating through the diverse cities, each chapter unfolding a new layer of our journey. It's a literary voyage."

Aaron, enthusiastically, replies "Yes, and interspersed with our personal reflections, we delve into the historical and cultural context of each city, offering readers a multifaceted experience. The Colosseum isn't just a monument; it's a testament to centuries of human endeavour."

Avan, smirking, adds "You have a way with words, Aaron. Our narrative is rich with vivid descriptions and eloquent prose, inviting readers to taste the gelato in Venice and feel the cobblestones beneath their feet in Verona."

Aaron, grinning, says "Language is our brush, painting a canvas of emotions. And let's not forget the dialogues—conversations like the ones we're having now, capturing the essence of our camaraderie."

Avan, raising an eyebrow, starts to react "Dialogues that echo the laughter, the debates, and the quiet moments of reflection. Our book makes readers feel like they're sipping espresso with us in a Roman cafe."

Aaron, leaning in, speaks out "Avan, let's make it more than a travelogue; let's make it a celebration of friendship and discovery. A journey not just through Italy but through the intricacies of our connection."

Avan, smiling, replies "Agreed. Our story resonates beyond the pages, leaving an imprint on the hearts of those who read it. It's a shared endeavour, Aaron—a literary reflection of our Italian sojourn."

As time passes, the outlines of their book take shape amidst the clinking of cutlery and the distant murmur of the restaurant. The candle's glow mirrors the spark of creativity between Aaron and Avan, two kindred spirits weaving their journey into a narrative that transcends time—a testament to the enduring magic of their friendship. But yet it is only an idea and they are not sure whether they will make it real or not. Who knows, maybe one day, but not very soon, not so soon. They both wait impatiently to see their book. They both cross their fingers for that opportunity.

Chapter Nine

<u>THIS BOOK'S FINALE</u>
<u>ENDINGS ARE JUST THE START OF SOMETHING NEW</u>
<u>SOMETHINGS ARE BETTER LATE THAN NEVER</u>

It is first thing in the morning a bit after sunrise, and Avan and Aaron are seated in a breakfast nook in the corner of a sunny, bustling cafe. A flock of birds from Mercato Centrale are whistling in the distance, heightening the pleasantness of the atmosphere. Streams of sunlight are gushing through the glass window panes. They have since returned to Florence. The floor of the cafe is covered in Amalfi ceramic tiles that are so shiny they could have been glazed. An orchestra of subtle and bright sounds was like a score behind Avan and Aaron. However, as many locals, taxi drivers, and shop owners recently discovered, nothing could detract from the pair's conversations or divert their attention. Each long-winded discussion or heated debate, even when they took turns pontificating, could not be interrupted. They were holding on to each other's words like a cactus holding on to a few drops of water in the desert to bloom. At a quick glance, it almost looked as though they were serious competitors, and they would be if they could keep a straight face. Because after a certain number of cigarettes, coffees, and glasses of prosecco, of course, they were propelled to their fate of collapsing into laughter. Avan secretly knew Aaron was the only person in the world who could make her laugh so hard tears streamed down her cheeks. Their jokes could be silly, smart, dark, cheeky, even through any tension they came across when it came to reading maps, or what to have for dinner, or which was the best route back to the hotel– (Aaron preferred looking at a map or google maps, while Avan preferred trying to get back without either) it could easily be resolved, even a mountain of conflict, with a bit of Aaron's wit, kindness, patience, and sideways humour.

Sounds of coffee cups being set down on saucers, clinks of forks and knives, bits and pieces of morning gossip and chatter, and the whirring of the espresso machine and boiling water circulated around Aaron and Avan like the strong aroma of coffee beans being ground up into a fine powder. They are at the coffee shop early enough where only older couples are there for an espresso and the cafe's famous sfogliatina (sweet puff pastries) and pistachio cannolis. The past few days of travel are indeed noticeable on their exhausted but happy faces. And at that moment, they both pause to take a sip of coffee. Avan's usual flawless appearance is now anything but; her mussed hair is tangled and hidden under a Chicago Cubs baseball hat. Aaron's button-down shirt is rolled up several times to hide the sleeve that he accidentally ripped on that Gondola boat tour in Venice. To pack as much into their days as possible, there were many nights that Avan and Aaron decided to forgo several hours of sleep, and that exchange was visible on their faces. Dark circles are under their eyes but they are also big, satisfied, and a bit coy smiles. There is a moment of truth that emerges after a long time, perhaps one they already know but were too frightened to speak aloud. Avan thought to herself as she sipped her searing hot coffee, *I am sitting next to my soul mate, and there is no one and nowhere else in the world I would rather be sitting adjacent to.* It is as if these days of travel reminded Avan, with Aaron's help, who she is, at her core. She felt happy, like bubbles or a rainbow, an ephemeral burst of colour and light.

They made their way back to Florence in a circle, after tiptoeing out of the family wedding, because other exotic places in Italy were calling their names. Rome, the Vatican, Venice, and then back to Florence. They took turns with the Canon DSLR camera that Avan brought, and for the first time ever, Avan had yet to see what pictures were on her camera. She is waiting to make it a surprise. She is curious about what Aaron decides to capture and how the pictures will turn out. They did not intend to cultivate a mystique with Avan's family. They said their hellos, danced a bit, introduced Aaron to her family, and soaked in the views. Staying any longer would have been superfluous. The open road was calling, and they just wanted to savour each second in this magnificent country. They made their way to Rome first, and even though neither of them was too religious, the Vatican felt too big to not see. It was impressive, to say the least, indescribable, beyond words. The time that went into making it what it is. The gold, the details, the painting, the

54

architecture, the fact that Vatican City is the smallest country in the world, the fact that despite neither of them being part of Catholicism as a religion but being deeply moved by the history of it all added to it. A piece of history near the Pope, the first place to check off their list.

"Avan, where on earth is your mind?" Aaron teased, as Avan was staring off into the distance, motionless.

"Oh, sorry, I was just daydreaming about the past few days," Avan snapped out of it sheepishly.

"We can reminisce all we want shortly after this."

"Shortly after what?"

"Here. I got this for you." Aaron took a small box out of his knapsack and carefully placed it on the table.

"For me!" Avan could not believe it. They had been inseparable for the past few days, how and where did Aaron have time to buy her a gift without her noticing?

Avan took out a couple of boxes from her purse as well and slowly pushed them across to Aaron.

"Sorry, I wrapped them in newspaper since I could not find any wrapping paper!"

"Do not worry, it matters more what is inside than what you wrapped it with. Although I am sure you know by now I don't speak Italian?" Aaron laughed.

"You could have fooled me with the way you were trying to talk to that waitress in Venice! And well, now you can start learning Italian, and you can start by translating La Nazione, and this headline: Morti nello schianto a Barberino, l'ora del dolore. Ester, Edo e Leonardo: vite spezzate[1]!" Avan jokes, leaning closer to the gift, taking off her specs and squinting to read the newsprint whilst horribly mispronouncing the words.

"You and me both, we can learn Italian together. Since you already know Spanish, I am sure it will not be as difficult for you as it will be for me." Aaron suddenly has a twinge of melancholy in his voice.

Avan swallows, her voice now uncharacteristically quiet.

"Aaron, do you mind if I open this gift later?" The tone of Avan's voice is shaky and high-pitched.

"No problem, though you know you are supposed to open it now?"

"If I open this, that is our goodbye. And as Marjane Satrapi wrote in Persepolis, 'Nothing's worse than saying goodbye. It's a little like dying.'"

"Avan, I have been thinking about it over the past few days, and I really cannot imagine my life without you. I have loved every minute of sharing these travels with you. But my point...my point is that you mean a lot to me, and in a few short days, you have made my life worth living, more hopeful, more sparkly. I hope I have done the same for you. I know there is a lot to figure out about the future, but what do you think about sharing the future together, with me? It's taken me ten years to say this out loud, and even with the risk of sounding trite, I want to tell you that I love you, that I have always loved you. You are the only person I have ever truly loved, and I want to share the future with you. Life is short, and I want to prioritise my own happiness, which I feel is our happiness. I'm in if you're in. What do you say?"

Avan is smiling and crying and has melted in front of Aaron. She has waited years to hear these words, she can't believe it. This was only supposed to be a trip to her cousin Hannah's wedding, not her own sideways, unexpected love story. All she ever wanted was for Aaron to be happy, and she was never certain if Aaron felt as strongly or deeply as she felt about him. A velvety feeling of relief mixed with happiness gave Avan goosebumps.

"What took you so long?" Avan smiled through her tears. "I love you more than I love the moon."

Aaron, nervously sipping his Americano, musters the courage to express his feelings to Avan. "Avan," he says, looking into Avan's eyes, "that was something I've been wanting to tell you for a while now. I think I've fallen for you. I do believe that it is quite natural and normal for a human being"

Avan, pleasantly surprised, smiles and replies, "Aaron, I never expected this, but I must say, I'm glad you feel that way. I've been feeling the same."

---

1.   https://www.lanazione.it/firenze/cronaca/incidente-mortale-barberino-523d74f8

As they bask in the newfound warmth of their emotions, the conversation naturally flows into tales of love and romance. Avan, stirring his espresso, begins, "You know, love is like a delicate dance. It's a waltz of emotions, twirling us around and sometimes catching us off guard."

Aaron nods in agreement, adding, "Absolutely, Avan. It's like navigating a maze. You never know what twists and turns await, but there's something exhilarating about the journey."

Their conversation unfolds like a symphony of words blending seamlessly with the clinking of cups and the murmur of other patrons. Avan shares a story of a childhood crush that has blossomed into a lifelong friendship, describing it as a slow-burning flame that endures the test of time.

Aaron, leaning back in his chair, chimes in, "I once read somewhere that love is like a rollercoaster. It has its ups and downs, and it's a thrilling ride if you're willing to hold on tight."

Avan chuckles, "That's a vivid metaphor, Aaron. Love is indeed an adventure, full of unexpected twists and turns. Sometimes, you just have to enjoy the ride and embrace the unpredictability."

As the conversation deepens, they discuss the idiosyncrasies of relationships and the universal truth that love knows no boundaries. Aaron expresses, "Love, Avan, is like a universal language. It transcends cultural differences and connects us on a profound level."

Avan nods thoughtfully, "You're right, Aaron. It's a language that speaks to the soul, allowing us to understand and be understood in ways words alone can't convey."

Their time together in that cosy coffee shop in Florence becomes a chapter in their unfolding love story. They savour the rich blend of coffee and conversation, their connection growing stronger with each shared tale, and laughter echoing through the charming surroundings.

As the sun dips below the Tuscan horizon, casting a romantic hue over the city, Avan and Aaron leave the coffee shop hand in hand, ready to explore the chapters of their own love story, written in the language of the heart.

As Avan and Aaron stroll through the enchanting streets of Florence, the historic architecture whispers tales of centuries past. The rhythmic sound of their footsteps echoes the melody of their hearts.

The sun dips lower, painting the sky with hues of amber and lavender. Avan and Aaron find themselves in a small piazza, surrounded by the soft glow of street lamps. It is there, amidst the timeless beauty of the city, that they acknowledge the reality of their separate paths. But nothing is impossible, and love is forever a worthy cause.

Aaron, looking into Avan's eyes, sighs, "Avan, these moments with you are incredible."

As they continue to walk, the city's lights begin to twinkle, mirroring the stars that adorn the night sky. The lively chatter of people in nearby cafes and the distant strains of music add to the poignant atmosphere.

They decide to make the most of their last night together, savouring the sights and sounds of Florence. They wander through the narrow streets, pausing at a gelato stand to indulge in the flavours of Italy. The taste of pistachio and tiramisu becomes a bittersweet memory etched in their minds.

Laughter, music, and the aroma of delicious food fill the air. Avan and Aaron are together finally, which is all that matters.

The stars overhead seem to reflect the unspoken sadness in their eyes that was created from the years they spent apart.

As the night wears on, Avan and Aaron steal quiet moments away from the celebration. They find solace in each other's arms at last.

Beneath the Tuscan moon, they embrace, silently promising to carry the essence of their time together across continents and knowing that tomorrow they will figure out how to spend the rest of their lives together.

As Avan leaves the vibrant celebration behind, making her way through the quiet streets, she carries with her the echoes of laughter, the taste of gelato, and the warmth of a true love discovered in the heart of Florence. The city, witness to their profound connection, watches silently as they embark on a new journey, their two hearts now one.

In this romantic city centre, Avan and Aaron embark on a leisurely stroll through the streets. The city lights flicker like stars, casting a romantic glow on the cobblestone pathways.

As they walk side by side, their conversation meanders through the labyrinth of romantic musings. Avan, with a grin, remarks, "You know, Aaron, they say love is a journey, not a destination. It's all about enjoying the walk, isn't it?"

Aaron nods in agreement, "Absolutely, Avan. It's like we're on this adventurous path, encountering twists and turns. Who knows what surprises await?"

Avan, glancing around at the city's vibrant energy, adds, "And they say when you least expect it, love comes knocking on your door. Just like this city, full of surprises."

Their laughter echoes through the urban landscape as they continue their exploration. Aaron, with a playful twinkle in his eye, says, "Avan, they also say love is like a box of chocolates – you never know what you're gonna get. It's the unpredictability that makes it exciting."

Avan chuckles, "True, Aaron. It's like unwrapping a mystery every day, discovering new layers and flavours."

As they walk past charming cafes and under arching bridges, the city becomes a backdrop to their unfolding story. Avan, leaning against a stone railing, looks at Aaron and says, "You know, they say the best things in life are free. Like this moment, just you and me, sharing these romantic thoughts."

Aaron nods, "Indeed, Avan. They also say actions speak louder than words. Maybe it's time to let our actions do the talking."

With that, Aaron gently takes Avan's hand, and they continue their journey through the city, their connection deepening with every step. The night air is filled with the buzz of the city, and their hearts beat in harmony with the urban rhythm.

As the clock strikes midnight, they find themselves at a picturesque bridge overlooking the shimmering river. The city lights reflect in the water, creating a magical ambience. Avan, looking into Aaron's eyes, says, "You know, Aaron, they say all good things must come to an end. But endings are just the start of something new."

The stars above whisper tales of love that transcend the boundaries of time and distance. Avan and Aaron are a testament that love knows no bounds, and things are better late than never.

ENDINGS ARE JUST THE START OF SOMETHING NEW. ESPECIALLY WHEN IT COMES TO LOVE. THE BEST THINGS ARE WORTH THE WAIT.

-The END (for NOW ONLY)-

Authors' Bios:

Meet Areen Ahmed Muhammed, a dynamic figure seamlessly navigating the realms of academia and literature. Serving as a University Lecturer, Areen imparts knowledge to eager minds while also making significant strides in the literary world. With two compelling novels already under his belt, Areen's storytelling prowess transcends the written word; he is also a Motivational Speaker, inspiring audiences with his insights on personal growth and resilience. As he unveils his third novel, Areen continues to embody the fusion of academia and creativity, offering readers a captivating exploration of the human experience and leaving an enduring impact on both the academic and literary landscapes. He has PhD degree and is currently an assistant professor in English Language. He is living in Sulaymaniya, Kurdistan.

Find more about him on Instagram

(@Areen.Muhammed)

Ava Ginsburg is a 30-year-old writer (by 2024), filmmaker, and photographer based in Chicago, Illinois, USA. She graduated with a BFA in Film Production from Columbia in 2016. She enjoys reading, bicycling, watching films, and drinking coffee in her free time. She has a cat named Q-tip. She loves Antonín Dvořák, bunnies, and travelling.

Your Notes:

Your Memoir:

Your Diary:

Your Story and Words:

Dusky Embrace Areen & Ava